*A bestselling sensation here, there,
and now everywhere, Terry Pratchett's
profoundly irreverent novels are like
nothing you've ever experienced before.
Discover the world of Terry Pratchett.
It's a lot like our own.
Only different.*

Outstanding Acclaim for Terry Pratchett

"Very, very funny."
The Times (London)

"Pratchett's Monty Python-like plots are almost
impossible to describe. His talent for
characterization and dialogue and
his pop-culture allusions steal the show."
Chicago Tribune

"Trying to summarize the plot of a Pratchett novel
is like describing *Hamlet* as a play about
a troubled guy with an Oedipus complex

"Superb popular entertainment."
Washington Post Book World

"Pratchett has now moved beyond the limits of
humorous fantasy, and should be recognized as
one of the more significant contemporary
English language satirists."
Publishers Weekly

"Consistently, inventively mad . . .
wild and wonderful!"
Isaac Asimov's Science Fiction Magazine

"Think J.R.R. Tolkien with a
sharper, more satiric edge."
Houston Chronicle

"Discworld takes the classic fantasy universe
through its logical, and comic, evolution."
Cleveland Plain Dealer

"Truly original. . . . Discworld is more complicated
and satisfactory than Oz. . . . Has the energy of
The Hitchhiker's Guide to the Galaxy and the
inventiveness of *Alice in Wonderland*. . . . Brilliant."
A.S. Byatt

Terry Pratchett

EriC
A Novel of Discworld®

HarperTorch
An Imprint of HarperCollinsPublishers

First published in Great Britain 1990 by Victor Gollancz Ltd

HARPERTORCH
An Imprint of HarperCollins*Publishers*
10 East 53rd Street
New York, New York 10022-5299

First HarperTorch paperback printing: February 2002

HarperCollins®, HarperTorch™, and ❦™ are trademarks of HarperCollins Publishers Inc.

Printed in the United States of America

Visit HarperTorch on the World Wide Web at
www.harpercollins.com

10 9

Eric

~~**Faust**~~

13 Midden Lane,
    Pseudopolis,
    Sto Plains,
    The Discworld,
    On top of Great
A'tuin,
        The Univers,
    Space.
    nr. More Space.

The bees of Death are big and black, they buzz low and somber, they keep their honey in combs of wax as white as altar candles. The honey is black as night, thick as sin and sweet as treacle.

It is well known that eight colors make up white. But there are also eight colors of blackness, for those that have the seeing of them, and the hives of Death are among the black grass in the black orchard under the black-blossomed, ancient boughs of trees that will, eventually, produce apples that . . . put it like this . . . probably won't be red.

The grass was short now. The scythe that had done the work leaned against the gnarled bole of a pear tree. Now Death was inspecting his bees, gently lifting the combs in his skeletal fingers.

A few bees buzzed around him. Like all beekeepers, Death wore a veil. It wasn't that he had anything to sting, but sometimes a bee would get inside his skull and buzz around and give him a headache.

As he held a comb up to the gray light of his lit-

1

tle world between the realities there was the faintest of tremors. A hum went up from the hive, a leaf floated down. A wisp of wind blew for a moment through the orchard, and that was the most uncanny thing, because the air in the land of Death is always warm and still.

Death fancied that he heard, very briefly, the sound of running feet and a voice saying, no, a voice thinking *oshitoshitoshit, I'm gonna die I'm gonna die I'm gonna DIE!*

Death is almost the oldest creature in the universe, with habits and modes of thought that mortal man cannot begin to understand, but because he was also a good beekeeper he carefully replaced the comb in its rack and put the lid on the hive before reacting.

He strode back through the dark garden to his cottage, removed the veil, carefully dislodged a few bees who had got lost in the depths of his cranium, and retired to his study.

As he sat down at his desk there was another rush of wind, which rattled the hour-glasses on the shelves and made the big pendulum clock in the hall pause ever so briefly in its interminable task of slicing time into manageable bits.

Death sighed, and focused his gaze.

There is nowhere Death will not go, no matter how distant and dangerous. In fact the more dangerous it is, the more likely he is to be there already.

Now he stared through the mists of time and space.

OH, he said. IT'S HIM.

It was a hot afternoon in late summer in Ankh-Morpork, normally the most thriving, bustling and above all the most crowded city on the Disc. Now the spears of the sun had achieved what innumerable invaders, several civil wars and the curfew law had never achieved. It had pacified the place.

Dogs lay panting in the scalding shade. The river Ankh, which never what you might call sparkled, oozed between its banks as if the heat had sucked all the spirit out of it. The streets were empty, oven-brick hot.

No enemies had ever taken Ankh-Morpork. Well, *technically* they had, quite often; the city welcomed free-spending barbarian invaders, but somehow the puzzled raiders always found, after a few days, that they didn't own their own horses

3

anymore, and within a couple of months they were just another minority group with its own graffiti and food shops.

But the heat had besieged the city and triumphed over the walls. It lay over the trembling streets like a shroud. Under the blowlamp of the sun assassins were too tired to kill. It turned thieves honest. In the ivy-covered fastness of Unseen University, premier college of wizardry, the inmates dozed with their pointy hats over their faces. Even bluebottles were too exhausted to bang against windowpanes. The city siesta'd, awaiting the sunset and the brief, hot, velvet surcease of the night.

Only the Librarian was cool. He was also swinging and hanging out.

This was because he'd rigged up a few ropes and rings in one of the sub-basements of the Unseen University Library—the one where they kept the, um, erotic* books. In vats of crushed ice. And he was dreamily dangling in the chilly vapor above them.

---

*Just erotic. Nothing kinky. It's the difference between using a feather and using a chicken.

All books of magic have a life of their own. Some of the really energetic ones can't simply be chained to the bookshelves; they have to be nailed shut or kept between steel plates. Or, in the case of the volumes on tantric sex magic for the serious connoisseur, kept under very cold water to stop them from bursting into flames and scorching their severely plain covers.

The Librarian swung gently back and forth above the seething vats, dozing peacefully.

Then the footsteps came out of nowhere, raced across the floor with a noise that scraped the raw surface of the soul, and disappeared through the wall. There was a faint, distant scream that sounded like *ogodsogodsogods, this is IT, I'm gonna DIE*.

The Librarian woke up, lost his grip, and flopped into the few inches of tepid water that was all that stood between *The Joy of Tantric Sex with Illustrations for the Advanced Student*, by A Lady, and spontaneous combustion.

And it would have gone badly for him if the Librarian had been a human being. Fortunately, he was currently an orangutan. With so much raw magic sloshing around in the Library it would be

5

surprising if accidents did not happen sometimes, and one particularly impressive one had turned him into an ape. Not many people get the chance to leave the human race while still alive, and he'd strenuously resisted all efforts since to turn him back. Since he was the only librarian in the universe who could pick up books with his feet, the University hadn't pressed the point.

It also meant that his idea of desirable female companionship now looked something like a sack of butter thrown through a roll of old inner tubes, and so he was lucky to get away with only mild burns, a headache, and some rather ambivalent feelings about cucumbers, which wore off by teatime.

In the Library above, the grimoires creaked and rustled their pages in astonishment as the invisible runner passed straight through the bookshelves and disappeared, or rather, disappeared even more . . .

Ankh-Morpork gradually awoke from its slumber. Something invisible and yelling at the top of its voice was passing through every part of the city, dragging in its wake a trail of destruction. Wherever it went, things changed.

A fortune-teller in the Street of Cunning Artificers heard the footsteps run across her bedroom floor and found her crystal ball had turned into a little glass sphere with a cottage in it, plus snowflakes.

In a quiet corner of the Mended Drum tavern, where the adventuresses Herrena the Henna-Haired Harridan, Red Scharron and Diome, Witch of the Night, were meeting for some girl talk and a game of canasta, all the drinks turned into small yellow elephants.

"It's them wizards up at the University," said the barman, hastily replacing the glasses. "It oughtn't to be allowed."

Midnight dropped off the clock.

The Council of Wizardry rubbed their eyes and stared blearily at one another. They felt it oughtn't to be allowed too, especially since they weren't the ones that were allowing it.

Finally the new Archchancellor, Ezrolith Churn, suppressed a yawn, sat up straight in his chair, and tried to look suitably magisterial. He knew he wasn't really Archchancellor material. He hadn't really wanted the job. He was ninety-eight, and had achieved this worthwhile age by carefully not being any trouble or threat to anyone. He had hoped to spend his twilight years completing his seven-volume treatise on *Some Little Known Aspects of Kuian Rain-making Rituals*, which were an ideal subject for academic study in his opinion since the rituals only ever worked in Ku, and that particular continent had slipped into the ocean several thousand years ago.* The trouble was that in recent years the lifespan of Archchancellors seemed to be a bit on the short side, and the natural ambition of all wizards for the job had given way to a curious, self-effacing politeness. He'd come down one morning to find everyone calling him "sir." It had taken him days to find out why.

His head ached. He felt it was several weeks past his bedtime. But he had to say something.

"Gentlemen—" he began.

"Oook."

---

*It took thirty years to subside. The inhabitants spent a lot of the time wading. It went down in history as the multiverse's most embarrassing continental catastrophe.

"Sorry, *and* mo—"

"*Oook.*"

"I mean apes, of course—"

"*Oook.*"

The Archchancellor opened and shut his mouth in silence for a while, trying to re-route his train of thought. The Librarian was, ex officio, a member of the college council. No one had been able to find any rule about orang-utans being barred, although they had surreptitiously looked very hard for one.

"It's a haunting," he ventured. "Some sort of a ghost, maybe. A bell, book and candle job."

The Bursar sighed. "We tried that, Archchancellor."

The Archchancellor leaned toward him.

"Eh?" he said.

"I *said*, we tried that, Archchancellor," said the Bursar loudly, directing his voice at the old man's ear. "After dinner, you remember? We used Humptemper's *Names of the Ants* and rang Old Tom."*

"Did we, indeed. Worked, did it?"

---

*Old Tom was the single cracked bronze bell in the University bell tower. The clapper dropped out shortly after it was cast, but the bell still tolled out some tremendously sonorous silences every hour.

"*No*, Archchancellor."

"Eh?"

"Anyway, we've never had any trouble with ghosts before," said the Senior Tutor. "Wizards just don't haunt places."

The Archchancellor groped for a crumb of comfort.

"Perhaps it's just something natural," he said. "Possibly the rumblings of an underground spring. Earth movements, perhaps. Something in the drains. They can make very funny noises, you know, when the wind is in the right direction."

He sat back and beamed.

The rest of the council exchanged glances.

"The drains don't sound like hurrying feet, Archchancellor," said the Bursar wearily.

"Unless someone left a tap running," said the Senior Tutor.

The Bursar scowled at him. He'd been in the tub when the invisible screaming thing had hurtled through his room. It was not an experience he wanted to repeat.

The Archchancellor nodded at him.

"That's settled, then," he said, and fell asleep.

The Bursar watched him in silence. Then he pulled the old man's hat off and tucked it gently under his head.

"Well?" he said wearily. "Has anyone got any suggestions?"

The Librarian put his hand up.

"Oook," he said.

"Yes, well done, good boy," said the Bursar, breezily. "Anyone else?"

The orang-utan glared at him as the other wizards shook their heads.

"It's a tremor in the texture of reality," said the Senior Tutor. "That's what it is."

"What should we do about it, then?"

"Search me. Unless we tried the old—"

"Oh, no," said the Bursar. "Don't say it. Please. It's far too dangerous—"

His words were chopped off by a scream that began at the far end of the room and dopplered along the table, accompanied by the sound of many running feet. The wizards ducked in a scatter of overturned chairs.

The candle flames were drawn into long thin tongues of octarine light before being snuffed out.

11

Then there was silence, the special kind that you get after a really unpleasant noise.

And the Bursar said, "All right. I give in. We *will* try the Rite of AshkEnte."

It is the most serious ritual eight wizards can undertake. It summons Death, who naturally knows everything that is going on everywhere.

And of course it's done with reluctance, because senior wizards are generally very old and would prefer not to do anything to draw Death's attention in their direction.

It took place in the midnight in the University's Great Hall, in a welter of incense, candlesticks, runic inscriptions and magic circles, none of which was strictly necessary but which made the wizards feel better. Magic flared, the chants were chanted, the invocations were truly invoked.

The wizards stared into the magic octogram, which remained empty. After a while the circle of robed figures began to mutter among themselves.

"We must have done something wrong."

"Oook."

"Maybe He is out."

"Or busy . . ."

"Do you think we could give up and go back to bed?"

WHO ARE WE WAITING FOR, EXACTLY?

The Bursar turned slowly to the figure beside him. You could always tell a wizard's robe; it was bedecked with sequins, sigils, fur and lace, and there was usually a considerable amount of wizard inside it. This robe, however, was very black. The material looked as though it had been chosen for its hard-wearing qualities. So did its owner. He looked as though if he wrote a diet book, it would be a bestseller.

Death was watching the octogram with an expression of polite interest.

"Er," said the Bursar. "The fact is, in fact, that, er, you should be on the *inside*."

I'M SO SORRY.

Death stalked in a dignified way into the center of the room and watched the Bursar expectantly.

I HOPE WE ARE NOT GOING TO HAVE ANY OF THIS "FOUL FIEND" BUSINESS AGAIN, he said.

"I trust we are not interrupting any important enterprise?" said the Bursar politely.

ALL MY WORK IS IMPORTANT, said Death.

"Naturally," said the Bursar.

TO SOMEBODY.

"Er. Er. The reason, o fou—sir, that we have called you here, is for the reason—"

IT IS RINCEWIND.

"What?"

THE REASON YOU SUMMONED ME. THE ANSWER IS: IT IS RINCEWIND.

"But we haven't asked you the question yet!"

NEVERTHELESS. THE ANSWER IS: IT IS RINCEWIND.

"Look, what we want to know *is*, what's causing this outbreak of . . . oh."

Death pointedly picked invisible particles off the edge of his scythe.

The Archchancellor cupped a gnarled hand over his ear.

"What'd he say? Who's the fella with the stick?"

"It's Death, Archchancellor," said the Bursar patiently.

"Eh?"

"It's Death, sir. *You* know."

"Tell him we don't want any," said the old wizard, waving his stick.

The Bursar sighed. "We summoned him, Archchancellor."

"Is it? What'd we go and do that for? Bloody silly thing to do."

The Bursar gave Death an embarrassed grin. He was on the point of asking him to excuse the Archchancellor on account of his age, but realized that this would in the circumstances be a complete waste of breath.

"Are we talking about the wizard Rincewind? The one with the—" the Bursar gave a shudder— "horrible Luggage on legs? But he got blown up when there was all that business with the sourcerer, didn't he?"*

INTO THE DUNGEON DIMENSIONS. AND NOW HE IS TRYING TO GET BACK HOME.

---

*The Bursar was referring obliquely to the difficult occasion when the University very nearly caused the end of the world, and would in fact have done so had it not been for a chain of events involving Rincewind, a magic carpet and a half-brick in a sock. (See *Sourcery*.) The whole affair was very embarrassing to wizards, as it always is to people who find out afterward that they were on the wrong side all along,** and it was remarkable how many of the University's senior staff were now adamant that at the time they had been off sick, visiting their aunt, or doing research with the door locked while humming loudly and had had no idea of what was going on outside. There had been some desultory talk about putting up a statue to Rincewind but, by the curious alchemy that tends to apply in these sensitive issues, this quickly became a plaque, then a note on the Roll of Honor, and finally a motion of censure for being improperly dressed.

**ie, the one that lost.

"Can he do that?"

THERE WOULD NEED TO BE AN UNUSUAL CONJUNC-
TION OF CIRCUMSTANCES. REALITY WOULD NEED TO
BE WEAKENED IN CERTAIN UNEXPECTED WAYS.

"That isn't likely to happen, is it?" said the Bursar anxiously. People who have it on record that
they were visiting their aunt for two months are always nervous about people turning up who may
have mistakenly thought that they weren't, and
owing to some trick of the light might have believed they had seen them doing things that they
couldn't have been doing owing to being at their
aunt's.

IT WOULD BE A MILLION TO ONE CHANCE, said
Death. EXACTLY A MILLION TO ONE CHANCE.

"Oh," said the Bursar, intensely relieved. "Oh
dear. What a shame." He brightened up consider-
ably. "Of course, there's all the noise. But, unfortunately, I expect he won't survive for long."

THIS COULD BE THE CASE, said Death blandly. I
AM SURE, THOUGH, THAT YOU WOULD NOT WISH ME
TO MAKE A PRACTICE OF ISSUING DEFINITIVE STATE-
MENTS IN THIS FIELD.

"No! No, of course not," said the Bursar hurriedly. "Right. Well, many thanks. Poor chap.

What a great pity. Still, can't be helped. Perhaps we should be philosophical about these things."

PERHAPS YOU SHOULD.

"And we had better not keep you," the Bursar added politely.

THANK YOU.

"Goodbye."

BE SEEING YOU.

In fact the noise stopped just before breakfast. The Librarian was the only one unhappy about it. Rincewind had been his assistant and his friend, and was a good man when it came to peeling a banana. He had also been uniquely good at running away from things. He was not, the Librarian considered, the type to be easily caught.

There had probably been an unusual conjunction of circumstances.

That was a far more likely explanation.

There *had* been an unusual conjunction of circumstances.

By exactly a million to one chance there had been someone watching, studying, looking for the right tools for a special job.

And here was Rincewind.

It was almost too easy.

So Rincewind opened his eyes. There was a ceiling above him; if it was the floor, then he was in trouble.

So far, so good.

He cautiously felt the surface he was lying on. It was grainy, woody in fact, with the odd nail-hole. A *human* sort of surface.

His ears picked up the crackle of a fire and a bubbling noise, source unknown.

His nose, feeling that it was being left out of things, hastened to report a whiff of brimstone.

Right. So where did that leave him? Lying on a rough wooden floor in a firelit room with something that bubbled and gave off sulfurous smells. In his unreal, dreamy state he felt quite pleased at this process of deduction.

What else?

Oh, yes.

He opened his mouth and screamed and screamed and screamed.

This made him feel slightly better.

He lay there a bit longer. Through the tumbled

heap of his memories came the recollections of mornings in bed when he was a little boy, desperately subdividing the passing time into smaller and smaller units to put off the terrible moment of getting up and having to face all the problems of life such as, in this case, who he was, where he was, and why he was.

"*What* are you?" said a voice on the edge of his consciousness.

"I was coming to that," muttered Rincewind.

The room oscillated into focus as he pushed himself up on his elbows.

"I warn you," said the voice, which seemed to be coming from a table, "I am protected by many powerful amulets."

"Jolly good," said Rincewind. "I wish I was."

Details began to distil out of the blur. It was a long, low room, one end of which was entirely occupied by an enormous fireplace. A bench all down one wall contained a selection of glassware apparently created by a drunken glassblower with hiccups, and inside its byzantine coils colored liquids seethed and bubbled. A skeleton hung from a hook in a relaxed fashion. On a perch beside it someone had nailed a stuffed bird. Whatever sins it had committed in life, it hadn't deserved what the taxidermist had done to it.

Rincewind's gaze then swept across the floor. It was obvious that it was the only sweeping the floor had had for some time. Only around him had space been cleared among the debris of broken glass and overturned retorts for—

A magic circle.

It looked an extremely thorough job. Whoever had chalked it was clearly very aware that its purpose was to divide the universe into two bits, the inside and the outside.

Rincewind was, of course, inside.

"Ah," he said, feeling a familiar and almost comforting sense of helpless dread sweep over him.

"I adjure and conjure thee against all aggressive acts, o demon of the pit," said the voice from, Rincewind now realized, *behind* the table.

"Fine, fine," said Rincewind quickly. "That's all right by me. Er. It isn't possible that there has been the *teeniest* little mistake here, could there?"

"Avaunt!"

"Right!" said Rincewind. He looked around him desperately. "How?"

"Don't you think you can lure me to my doom with thy lying tongue, o fiend of Shamharoth," said the table. "I am learned in the ways of demons. Obey my every command or I will return thee unto the boiling hell from which you came. Thou came, sorry. Thou came'st, in fact. And I really mean it."

The figure stepped out. It was quite short, and most of it was hidden by a variety of charms, amulets and talismans which, even if not effective against magic, would probably have protected it against a tolerably determined sword thrust. It wore glasses and had a hat with long sidepieces that gave it the air of a short-sighted spaniel.

It held a sword in one shaking hand. It was so heavily etched with sigils that it was beginning to bend.

"Boiling hell, did you say?" said Rincewind weakly.

"Absolutely. Where the screams of anguish and the tortured torments—"

"Yes, yes, you've made your point," said Rincewind. "Only, you see, the thing is, in fact, that I am not a demon. So if you would just let me out?"

21

"I am not fooled by thy outer garb, demon," said the figure. In a more normal voice it added, "Anyway, demons always lie. Well-known fact."

"It is?" said Rincewind, clutching at this straw. "In that case, then—I *am* a demon."

"Aha! Condemned out of your own mouth!"

"Look, I don't have to put up with this," said Rincewind. "I don't know who you are or what's happening, but I'm going to have a drink, all right?"

He went to walk out of the circle, and went rigid with shock as sparks crackled up from the runic inscriptions and earthed themselves all over his body.

"Thou mays'nt—thou maysn't—thou mays'n't—" The conjurer of demons gave up. "Look, you can't step over the circle until I release you, right? I mean, I don't want to be unpleasant, it's just that if I let you out of the circle you will be able to resume your true shape, and a pretty awful shape it is too, I expect. Avaunt!" he added, feeling that he wasn't keeping up the tone.

"All right. I'm avaunting. I'm avaunting," said Rincewind, rubbing his elbow. "But I'm still not a demon."

"How come you answered the conjuration,

then? I suppose you just happened to be passing through the paranatural dimensions, eh?"

"Something like that, I think. It's all a bit blurred."

"Pull the other one, it has got bells on." The conjurer leaned his sword against a lectern on which a heavy book, dripping bookmarks, lay open. Then he did a mad little jig on the floor.

"It's worked!" he said. "Heheh!" He caught sight of Rincewind's horrified gaze and pulled himself together. He gave an embarrassed cough, and stepped up to the lectern.

"I really am not—" Rincewind began.

"I had this list here somewhere," said the figure. "Let's see, now. Oh, yes. I command you—thee, I mean—to, ah, grant me three wishes. Yes. I want mastery of the kingdoms of the world, I want to meet the most beautiful woman who has ever lived, *and* I want to live forever." He gave Rincewind an encouraging look.

"All that?" said Rincewind.

"Yes."

"Oh, no problem," said Rincewind sarcastically. "And then I get the rest of the day off, right?"

"And I want a chest full of gold, too. Just to be going on with."

"I can see you've got it all thought out."

"Yes. Avaunt!"

"Right, right. Only—" Rincewind thought hurriedly, he's quite mad, but mad with a sword in his hands, the only chance I've got is to argue him out of it on his own terms, "—only, d'you see, I'm not a very superior kind of demon and I'm afraid those sort of errands are a bit out of my league, sorry. You can avaunt as much as you like, but they're just beyond me."

The little figure peered over the top of its glasses.

"I see," he said testily. "What could you manage then, do you think?"

"Well, er—" said Rincewind, "I suppose I could go down to the shops and get you a packet of mints, or something."

There was a pause.

"You really can't do all those things?"

"Sorry. Look, I'll tell you what. You just release me, and I'll be sure to pass the word around when I get back to—" Rincewind hesitated. Where the hell *did* demons live, anyway? "Demon City," he said, hopefully.

"You mean Pandemonium?" said his captor suspiciously.

"Yes, that's right. That's what I meant. I'll tell everyone, next time you're in the real world be sure and look up—what's your name?"

"Thursley. Eric Thursley."

"Right."

"Demonologist. Midden Lane, Pseudopolis. Next door to the tannery," said Thursley hopefully.

"Right you are. Don't you worry about it. Now, if you'll just let me out—"

Thursley's face fell.

"You're sure you really can't do it?" he said, and Rincewind couldn't help noticing the edge of pleading in his voice. "Even a small chest of gold would do. And, I mean, it needn't be the most beautiful woman in the whole of history. Second most beautiful would do. Or third. You pick any one out of, you know, the top one hundr—thousand. Whatever you've got in stock, sort of thing." By the end of the sentence his voice twanged with longing.

Rincewind wanted to say: Look, what you should do is stop all this messing around with chemicals in dark rooms and have a shave, a haircut, a bath, make that *two* baths, buy yourself a new wardrobe and get out of an evening and then—but he'd have to be honest, because even washed, shaved and soaked in body splash Thursley wasn't going to win any prizes—and then you could have your face slapped by any woman of your choice.

I mean, it wouldn't be much, but it would be body contact.

"Sorry," he said again.

Thursley sighed. "The kettle's on," he said. "Would you like a cup of tea?"

Rincewind stepped forward into a crackle of psychic energy.

"Ah," said Thursley uncertainly, as the wizard sucked at his fingers, "I'll tell you what. I'll put you under a conjuration of duress."

"There's no need, I assure you."

"No, it's best this way. It means you can move around. I had it all ready anyway, in case you could go and fetch, you know, *her*."

"Fine," said Rincewind. As the demonologist mumbled words from the book he thought: Feet. Door. Stairs. What a great combination.

It occurred to him that there was something

about the demonologist that wasn't quite usual, but he couldn't put his finger on it. He *looked* pretty much like the demonologists Rincewind had known back in Ankh-Morpork, who were all bent and chemical-stained and had eyes with pupils like pinheads from all the chemical fumes. This one would have fitted in easily. It was just that there was something odd.

"To be honest," said Thursley, industriously mopping away part of the circle, "you're my first demon. It's never worked before. What is your name?"

"Rincewind."

Thursley thought about this. "It doesn't ring a bell," he said. "There's a Riinjswin in the *Demonologie*. And a Winswin. But they've got more wings than you. You can step out now. I must say that's a first-class materialization. No one would think you were a fiend, to look at you. Most demons, when they want to look human, materialize in the shape of nobles, kings and princes. This moth-eaten-wizard look is very clever. You could've almost fooled me. It's a shame you can't do any of those things."

"I can't see why you'd want to live forever," said

Rincewind, privately determining that the words "moth-eaten" would be paid for, if ever he got the opportunity. "Being *young* again, I can understand that."

"Huh. Being young's not much fun," said Thursley, and then clapped his hand over his mouth.

Rincewind leaned forward.

About fifty years. *That* was what was missing.

"That's a false beard!" he said. "How old are you?"

"Eighty-seven!" squeaked Thursley.

"I can see the hooks over your ears!"

"Seventy-eight, honest! Avaunt!"

"You're a little boy!"

Eric pulled himself up haughtily. "I'm not!" he snapped. "I'm nearly fourteen!"

"Ah-*ha!*"

The boy waved the sword at Rincewind. "It doesn't matter, anyway!" he shouted. "Demonologists can be any age, you're still my demon and you have to do as I say!"

"*Eric!*" came a voice from somewhere below them.

Eric's face went white.

"Yes, Mother?" he shouted, his eyes fixed on Rincewind. His mouth shaped the words: don't say anything, *please*.

"What's all that noise up there?"

"Nothing, Mother!"

"Come down and wash your hands, dear, your breakfast's ready!"

"Yes, Mother." He looked sheepishly at Rincewind. "That's my mother," he said.

"She's got a good pair of lungs, hasn't she," said Rincewind.

"I'd, I'd better go, then," said Eric. "You'll have to stay up here, of course."

It dawned on him that he was losing a certain amount of credibility at this point. He waved the sword again.

"Avaunt!" he said. "I command you not to leave this room!"

"Right. Sure," said Rincewind, eyeing the windows.

"Promise? Otherwise you'll be sent back to the Pit."

"Oh, I don't want that," said Rincewind. "Off you trot. Don't worry about me."

"I'm going to leave the sword and stuff here,"

said Eric, removing most of his accoutrements to reveal a slim, dark-haired young man whose face would be a lot better when his acne cleared up. "If you touch them, terrible things will befall."

"Wouldn't dream of it," said Rincewind.

When he was left alone he wandered over to the lectern and looked at the book. The title, in impressively flickering red letters, was *Mallificarum Sumpta Diabolicite Occularis Singularum*, the Book of Ultimate Control. He knew about it. There was a copy in the Library somewhere, although wizards never bothered with it.

This might seem odd, because if there is one thing a wizard would trade his grandmother for, it is power. But it wasn't all *that* strange, because any wizard bright enough to survive for five minutes was also bright enough to realize that if there was any power in demonology, then it lay with the demons. Using it for your own purposes would be like trying to beat mice to death with a rattlesnake.

Even wizards thought demonologists were odd; they tended to be surreptitious, pale men who got up to complicated things in darkened rooms and had damp, weak handshakes. It wasn't like good clean magic. No self-respecting wizard would have any truck with the demonic regions, whose inhabitants were as big a collection of ding-dongs as you'd find outside a large belfry.

He inspected the skeleton closely, just in case. It didn't seem inclined to make a contribution to the situation.

"It belonged to his wossname, grandfather," said a cracked voice behind him.

"Bit of an unusual bequest," said Rincewind.

"Oh, not *personally*. He got it in a shop somewhere. It's one of them wossname, articulate wossnames."

"It's not saying much right now," said Rincewind, and then went very quiet and thoughtful.

"Er," he said, without moving his head, "what, precisely, am I talking to?"

"I'm a wossname. Tip of my tongue. Begins with a P."

Rincewind turned around slowly.

"You're a parrot?" he said.

"That's it."

Rincewind stared at the thing on the perch. It had one eye that glittered like a ruby. Most of the rest of it was pink and purple skin, studded with the fag-ends of feathers, so that the net effect was of an oven-ready hairbrush. It jiggled arthritically on its perch and then slowly lost its balance, until it was hanging upside down.

"I thought you were stuffed," said Rincewind.

"Up yours, wizard."

Rincewind ignored it and crept over to the window. It was small, but gave out onto a gently sloping roof. And out there was real life, real sky, real buildings. He reached out to open the shutters—

A crackling current coursed up his arm and earthed itself in his cerebellum.

He sat on the floor, sucking his fingers.

"He *tole* you," said the parrot, swinging backward and forward upside down. "But you wouldn't wossname. He's got you by the wossnames."

"But it should only work on demons!"

"Ah," said the parrot, achieving enough momentum to swing upright again, whereupon it steadied itself with the stubby remains of what had once been wings. "It's all according, isn't it. If you come in through the door marked 'Wossnames' that means you get treated as a wossname, right?

Demon, I mean. Subject to all the rules and woss-names. Tough one for you."

"But *you* know I'm a wizard, don't you!"

The parrot gave a squawk. "I've seen 'em, mate. The real McWossname. Some of the ones we've had in here, they'd make you choke on your millet. Great scaly fiery wossnames. Took weeks to get the soot off the walls," it added, in an approving tone of voice. "That was in his granddad's day, of course. The kid hasn't been any good at it. Up to now. Bright lad. I blame the wossnames, parents. New money, you know. Wine business. Spoil him rotten, let him play with his wossname's old stuff, 'Oh, he's *such* an intelligent lad, nose always in a book,'" the parrot mimicked. "They never give him any of the things a sensitive growing woss-name really needs, if you was to ask me."

"What, you mean love and guidance?" said Rincewind.

"I was thinking of a bloody good wossname, thrashing," said the parrot.

Rincewind clutched at his aching head. If this was what demons usually had to go through, no wonder they were always so annoyed.

33

"Polly want a biscuit," said the parrot vaguely, in much the same way as a human would say "Er" or "As I was saying," and went on, "His granddad was keen on it. That and his pigeons."

"Pigeons," said Rincewind.

"Not that he was particularly successful. It was all a bit trial and wossname."

"I thought you said great big scaly—"

"Oh, *yes*. But that wasn't what he was after. He was trying to conjure up a succubus." It should be impossible to leer when all you've got is a beak, but the parrot managed it. "That's a female demon what comes in the night and makes mad passionate wossn—"

"I've heard of them," said Rincewind. "Bloody dangerous things."

The parrot put its head on one side. "It never worked. All he ever got was a neuralger."

"What's that?"

"It's a demon that comes and has a headache at you."

Demons have existed on the Discworld for at least as long as the gods, who in many ways they closely resemble. The difference is basically the same as that between terrorists and freedom fighters.

Most of the demons occupy a spacious dimension close to reality, traditionally decorated in shades of flame and maintained at roasting point. This isn't actually necessary, but if there is one thing that your average demon is, it is a traditionalist.

In the center of the inferno, rising majestically from a lake of lava substitute and with unparalleled views of the Eight Circles, lies the city of Pandemonium.* At the moment, it was living up to its name.

Astfgl, the new King of the Demons, was furious. Not simply because the air-conditioning had

---

*Demons and their Hell are quite different from the Dungeon Dimensions, those endless parallel wastelands outside space and time. The sad, mad Things in the Dungeon Dimensions have no understanding of the world but simply crave light and shape and try to warm themselves by the fires of reality, clustering around it with about the same effect—if they ever broke through—as an ocean trying to warm itself around a candle. Whereas demons belong to the same space-time wossname, more or less, as humans, and have a deep and abiding interest in humanity's day-to-day affairs. Interestingly enough, the gods of the Disc have never bothered much about judging the souls of the dead, and so people only go to hell if that's where they believe, in their deepest heart, that they deserve to go. Which they won't do if they don't know about it. This explains why it is important to shoot missionaries on sight.

broken down again, not because he felt surrounded by idiots and plotters on every side, and not even because no one could pronounce his name properly yet, but also because he had just been given bad news. The demon who had been chosen by lottery to deliver it cowered in front of his throne with its tail between its legs. It was immortally afraid that something wonderful was soon going to happen to it.*

"It did *what*?" said Astfgl.

"It, er, it opened, o lord. The circle in Pseudopolis."

"Ah. The clever boy. We have great hopes of him."

"Er. Then it closed again, lord." The demon shut its eyes.

"And who went through?"

"Er." The demon looked around at its colleagues, clustered at the far end of the mile-long throne room.

"I said, and who went through?"

"In point of fact, o lord—"

"Yes?"

---

*Demons have a distorted sense of values.

36

"We don't know. Someone."

"I gave orders, did I not, that when the boy succeeded the Duke Vassenego was to materialize unto him, and offer him forbidden pleasures and dark delights to bend him to Our will?"

The King growled. The problem with being evil, he'd been forced to admit, was that demons were not great innovatory thinkers and really needed the spice of human ingenuity. And he'd really been looking forward to Eric Thursley, whose brand of superintelligent gormlessness was a rare delight. Hell needed horribly bright, self-centered people like Eric. They were much better at being nasty than demons could ever manage.

"Indeed, lord," said the demon, "And the duke has been awaiting the summons there for years, shunning all other temptations, steadfastly and patiently studying the world of men—"

"So *where was he?*"

"Er. Call of supernature, Lord," the demon gabbled. "Hadn't turned his back for two minutes when—"

"And *someone* went through?"

"We're trying to find out—"

Lord Astfgl's patience, which in any case had the

tensile strength of putty, snapped at this point. That just about summed it up. He had the kind of subjects who used the words "find out" when they meant "ascertain." Damnation was too good for them.

"Get out," he whispered. "And I shall see to it that you get a commendation for this—"

"O master, I plead—"

"Get out!"

The King stamped along the glowing corridors to his private apartments.

His predecessors had favored shaggy hind legs and hoofs. Lord Astfgl had rejected all that sort of thing out of hand. He held that no one would ever get taken seriously by those stuck-up bastards in Dun manifestin when their rear end kept ruminating all the time, and so he favored a red silk cloak, crimson tights, a cowl with two rather sophisticated little horns on it, and a trident. The end kept dropping off the trident but, he felt, it was the sort of get-up in which a demon king could be taken seriously . . .

In the coolness of his chambers—oh, by all the gods or, rather, not by all the gods, it had taken him *ages* to get them up to some sort of civilized standard, his predecessors had been quite content just to lounge around and tempt people, they had never heard of executive stress—he gently lifted the cover off the Mirror of Souls and watched it flicker into life.

Its cool black surface was surrounded by an ornate frame, from which curls of greasy smoke constantly unfolded and drifted.

Your wish, master? it said.

"Show me the events around the Pseudopolis gate over the last hour," said the King, and settled down to watch.

After a while he went and looked up the name "Rincewind" in the filing cabinet he had recently had installed, in place of the distressingly-bound old ledgers that had been there; the system still needed ironing out, though, because the bewildered demons filed everything under P for People.

Then he sat watching the flickering pictures and absentmindedly played with the stuff on his desk, to soothe his nerves.

He had any amount of desk things: notepads with magnets for paperclips, handy devices for holding pens and those tiny jotters that always came in handy, incredibly funny statuettes with slogans like "You're the Boss!," and little chromium balls and spirals operated by a sort of ersatz and short-lived perpetual motion. No one looking at that desk could have any doubt that they were, in cold fact, truly damned.

"I *see*," said Lord Astfgl, setting a selection of shiny balls swinging with one tap of a talon.

He couldn't remember any demon called Rincewind. On the other hand, there were *millions* of the wretched things, swarming all over the place with no sense of order, and he hadn't yet had time to carry out a proper census and retire the unnecessary ones. This one seemed to have fewer appendages and more vowels in its name than most. But it *had* to be a demon.

Vassenego was a proud old fool, one of the elder demons who smiled and despised him and not-quite-obeyed him, just because the King'd worked hard over the millennia to get from humble beginnings to where he was today. He wouldn't put it past the old devil to do this on purpose, just to spite him.

Well, he'd have to see about that later. Send him a memo or something. Too late to do anything about it now. He'd have to take a personal interest.

Eric Thursley was too good a prospect to pass up. Getting Eric Thursley would really annoy the gods.

Gods! How he hated the gods! He hated the gods even more than he hated the old guard like Vassenego, even more than he hated humans. He'd thrown a little soirée last week, he'd put a lot of thought into it, he wanted to show that he was prepared to let bygones be bygones, work with them for a new, better and more efficient universe. He'd called it a "Getting to Know You!" party. There'd been sausages on sticks and everything, he'd done his best to make it nice.

They hadn't even bothered to answer the invitations. And he'd made a special point of putting RSVP on them.

"Demon?"

Eric peered around the door.

"What shape are you?" he said.

"Pretty poor shape," said Rincewind.

"I've brought you some food. You do eat, do you?"

Rincewind tried some. It was a bowl of cereal, nuts, and dried fruit. He didn't have any quarrel with any of that. It was just that somewhere in the preparation something had apparently done to these innocent ingredients what it takes a million gravities to do to a neutron star. If you died of eating this sort of thing they wouldn't have to bury you, they would just need to drop you somewhere where the ground was soft.

He managed to swallow it. It wasn't difficult. The trick would have been preventing it from heading downward.

"Lovely," he choked. The parrot did a splendid impersonation of someone being sick.

"I've decided to let you go," said Eric. "It's pretty pointless keeping you, isn't it."

"Absolutely."

"You haven't any powers at all?"

"Sorry. Dead failure."

"You don't *look* too demonic, come to think about it," said Eric.

"They never do. You can't trust them wossnames," chortled the parrot. It lost its balance again. "Polly want a biscuit," it said, upside down.

Rincewind spun around. "You stay out of this, beaky!"

There was a sound behind them, like the universe clearing its throat. The chalk marks of the magic circle grew terribly bright for a moment, became fiery lines against the scuffed planks, and something dropped out of the empty air and landed heavily on the floor.

It was a large, metal-bound chest. It had fallen on its curved lid. After a while it started to rock violently, and then it extended hundreds of little pink legs and with considerable effort flipped itself over.

Finally it shuffled around until it was watching the pair of them. It was all the more disconcerting because it was staring without having any eyes to do it with.

Eric moved first. He grasped the home-made magic sword, which flapped wildly.

"You *are* a demon!" he said. "I nearly believed you when you said you weren't!"

"Wheee!" said the parrot.

"It's just my Luggage," said Rincewind desperately. "It's a sort of . . . well, it goes everywhere with me, there's nothing demonic about it . . . er." He hesitated. "Not much, anyway," he finished lamely.

"Avaunt!"

"Oh, not again."

The boy looked at the open book. "My commands earlier resume," he said firmly. "The most beautiful woman who has ever lived, mastery of all the kingdoms of the world, and to live forever. Get on with it."

Rincewind stood frozen.

"Well, go on," said Eric. "You're supposed to disappear in a puff of smoke."

"Listen, do you think I can just snap my fingers—"

Rincewind snapped his fingers.

There was a puff of smoke.

Rincewind gave his fingers a long shocked stare, as one might regard a gun that has been hanging on the wall for decades and has suddenly gone off and perforated the cat.

"They've hardly ever done that before," he said.

He looked down.

"Aargh," he said, and closed his eyes.

It was a better world in the darkness behind his eyelids. If he tapped his foot he could persuade himself that he could *feel* the floor, he could know that he was really standing in the room, and that the urgent signals from all his other senses, which were telling him that he was suspended in the air some thousand miles or so above the Disc, were just a bad dream he'd wake up from. He hastily canceled that thought. If he was asleep he'd prefer to stay that way. You could *fly* in dreams. If he woke up, it was a long way to fall.

Perhaps I have died and I really am a demon, he thought.

It was an interesting point.

He opened his eyes again.

"*Wow!*" said Eric, his eyes gleaming. "Can I have *all* of it?"

The boy was standing in the same position as he had been in the room. So was the Luggage. So, to Rincewind's annoyance, was the parrot. It was perching in midair, looking speculatively at the cosmic panorama below.

The Disc might almost have been designed to be seen from space; it hadn't, Rincewind was damn sure, been designed to be lived on. But he had to admit that it was impressive.

The sun was about to rise on the far rim and made a line of fire that glittered around half the circumference. A long slow dawn was just beginning its sweep across the dark, massive landscape.

Below, harshly lit in the arid vacuum of space,

Great A'Tuin the world turtle toiled under the weight of Creation. On his—or her, the matter had never really been resolved—carapace the four giant elephants strained to support the Disc itself.

There might have been more efficient ways to build a world. You might start with a ball of molten iron and then coat it with successive layers of rock, like an old-fashioned gobstopper. And you'd have a very efficient planet, but it wouldn't look so nice. Besides, things would drop off the bottom.

"Pretty good," said the parrot. "Polly want a continent."

"It's so *big*," breathed Eric.

"Yes," said Rincewind flatly.

He felt that something more was expected of him.

"Don't break it," he added.

He had a nagging doubt about all this. If he was for the sake of argument a demon, and so many things had happened to him recently he was prepared to concede that he might have died and not noticed it in the confusion,* then he still didn't

---

*Rincewind had been told that death was just like going into another room. The difference is, when you shout, "Where's my clean socks?," no one answers.

46

quite see how the world was his to give away. He was pretty sure that it had owners who felt the same way.

Also, he was sure that a demon had to get something in writing.

"I think you have to sign for it," he said. "In blood."

"Whose?" said Eric.

"Yours, I think," said Rincewind. "Or bird blood will do, in a pinch." He glared meaningfully at the parrot, which growled at him.

"Aren't I allowed to try it out first?"

"What?"

"Well, supposing it doesn't work? I'm not signing for it until I've seen it work."

Rincewind stared at the boy. Then he looked down at the broad panorama of the kingdoms of the world. I wonder if I was like him at his age? he thought. I wonder how I survived?

"It's the world," he said patiently. "Of course it will bloody well work. I mean, *look* at it. Hurricanes, continental drift, rainfall cycle—it's all there. All ticking over like a bloody watch. It'll last you a lifetime, a world like that. Used carefully."

Eric gave the world a critical examination. He

wore the expression of someone who knows that all the best gifts in life seem to require the psychic equivalent of two U2 batteries and the shops won't be open until after the holidays.

"There's got to be tribute," he said flatly.

"What?"

"The kings of the world," said Eric. "They've got to pay me tribute."

"You've really been studying this, haven't you," said Rincewind sarcastically. "Just tribute? You don't fancy the moon while we're up here? This week's special offer, one free satellite with every world dominated?"

"Are there any useful minerals?"

"*What?*"

Eric gave a sigh of long-suffering patience.

"Minerals," he said. "Ores. You know."

Rincewind colored. "I don't think a lad your age should be thinking of—"

"I mean metal and things. It's no use to me if it's just a load of rock."

Rincewind looked down. The Discworld's tiny moonlet was just rising over the far edge, and shed a pale radiance across the jigsaw pattern of land and sea.

"Oh, I don't know. It looks quite nice," he volunteered. "Look, it's dark now. Perhaps everyone can pay you tribute in the morning?"

"I want some tribute *now*."

"I thought you might."

Rincewind gave his fingers a careful examination. It wasn't as if he'd ever been particularly good at snapping them.

He gave it another try.

When he opened his eyes again he was standing up to his ankles in mud.

Preeminent among Rincewind's talents was his skill in running away, which over the years he had elevated to the status of a genuinely pure science; it didn't matter if you were fleeing from or to, so long as you were fleeing. It was flight alone that counted. I run, therefore I am; more correctly, I run, therefore with any luck I'll still *be*.

But he was also skilled in languages and in practical geography. He could shout 'help!' in fourteen languages and scream for mercy in a further twelve. He had passed through many of the countries on the Disc, some of them at high speed, and during the long, lovely, *boring* hours when he'd worked in the Library he'd whiled away the time by reading up on all the exotic and faraway places he'd never visited. He remembered that at the time he'd sighed with relief that he'd never have to visit them.

And, now, here he was.

Jungle surrounded him. It wasn't nice, interesting, open jungle, such as leopard-skin-clad heroes might swing through, but serious, real jungle, jungle that towered up like solid slabs of greenness, thorned and barbed, jungle in which every representative of the vegetable kingdom had really rolled up its bark and got down to the strenuous business of outgrowing all competitors. The soil was hardly soil at all, but dead plants on the way to composthood; water dripped from leaf to leaf, insects whined in the humid, spore-laden air, and there was the terrible breathless silence made by the motors of photosynthesis running flat out. Any yodeling hero who tried to swing through that lot might just as well take his chances with a bean-slicer.

"How do you *do* that?" said Eric.

"It's probably a knack," said Rincewind.

Eric subjected the wonders of Nature to a cursory and disdainful glance.

"This doesn't look like a kingdom," he complained. "You said we could go to a kingdom. Do you call this a kingdom?"

"This is probably the rain forests of Klatch," said Rincewind. "They're stuffed full of lost kingdoms."

"You mean mysterious ancient races of Amazonian princesses who subject all male prisoners to strange and exhausting progenitative rites?" said Eric, his glasses beginning to fog.

"Haha," said Rincewind stonily. "What an imagination the child has."

"Wossname, wossname, wossname!" shrieked the parrot.

"I've read about them," said Eric, peering into the greenery. "Of course, I own those kingdoms as well." He stared at some private inner vision. "Gosh," he said, hungrily.

"I should concentrate on the tribute if I was you," said Rincewind, setting off down what was possibly a path.

The brightly colored blooms on a tree nearby turned to watch him go.

In the jungles of central Klatch there are, indeed, lost kingdoms of mysterious Amazonian princesses who capture male explorers for specifically masculine duties. These are indeed rigorous and exhausting and the luckless victims do not last long.*

There are also hidden plateaux where the reptilian monsters of a bygone epoch romp and play, as well as elephants' graveyards, lost diamond mines, and strange ruins decorated with hieroglyphs the very sight of which can freeze the most valiant heart. On any reasonable map of the area there's barely room for the trees.

The few explorers who have returned have passed on a number of handy hints to those who follow after, such as : 1) avoid if possible any hanging- down creepers with beady eyes and a forked tongue at one end; 2) don't pick up any orange-and-black-striped creepers that are apparently lying across the path, twitching, because there is often a tiger on the other end; and 3) don't go.

If I'm a demon, Rincewind thought hazily, why is everything stinging me and trying to trip me up? I mean, surely I can only be harmed by a wooden dagger through my heart? Or do I mean garlic?

---

*This is because wiring plugs, putting up shelves, sorting out the funny noise in attics and mowing lawns can eventually reduce even the strongest constitution.

Eventually the jungle opened out into a very wide, cleared area that stretched all the way to a distant blue range of volcanoes. The land fell away below them to a patchwork of lakes and swampy fields, here and there punctuated by great stepped pyramids, each one crowned with a thin plume of smoke curling into the dawn air. The jungle track opened out into a narrow, but paved, road.

"Where's this, demon?" said Eric.

"It looks like one of the Tezuman kingdoms," said Rincewind. "They're ruled over by the Great Muzuma, I think."

"She's an Amazonian princess, is she?"

"Strangely enough, no. You'd be astonished how many kingdoms aren't ruled by Amazonian princesses, Eric."

"It looks pretty primitive, anyway. A bit Stone Age."

"The Tezuman priests have a sophisticated calendar and an advanced horology," quoted Rincewind.

"Ah," said Eric, "Good."

"No," said Rincewind patiently. "It means time measurement."

"Oh."

53

"You'd approve of them. They're superb mathematicians, apparently."

"Huh," said Eric, blinking solemnly. "Shouldn't think they've got a lot to count in a backward civilization like this."

Rincewind eyed the chariots that were heading rapidly toward them.

"I think they usually count victims," he said.

The Tezuman Empire in the jungle valleys of central Klatch is known for its organic market gardens, its exquisite craftsmanship in obsidian, feathers and jade, and its mass human sacrifices in honor of Quezovercoatl, the Feathered Boa, god of mass human sacrifices. As they said, you always knew where you stood with Quezovercoatl. It was generally with a lot of people on top of a great stepped pyramid with someone in an elegant feathered headdress chipping an exquisite obsidian knife for your very own personal use.

The Tezumen are renowned on the continent for being the most suicidally gloomy, irritable and pessimistic people you could ever hope to meet, for reasons that may soon be made clear. It was true about the time measurement as well. The Tezumen had realized long ago that everything was steadily getting worse and, having a terrible literal-mindedness, had developed a complex system to keep track of how much worse each succeeding day was.

Contrary to general belief, the Tezumen *did* invent the wheel. They just had radically different ideas about what you used it for.

It was the first chariot Rincewind had ever seen that was pulled by llamas. That wasn't what was odd about it. What was odd about it was that it was being carried by people, two holding each side of the axle and running after the animals, their sandaled feet flapping on the flagstones.

"Do you think it's got the tribute in it?" said Eric.

All the leading chariot seemed to contain, apart from the driver, was a squat, basically cube-shaped man wearing a puma-skin outfit and a feather headdress.

The runners panted to a halt, and Rincewind saw that each man wore what would probably be described as a primitive sword, made by affixing shards of obsidian into a wooden club. They looked to him no less deadly than sophisticated, extremely civilized swords. In fact, they looked worse.

"Well?" said Eric.

"Well what?" said Rincewind.

"Tell him to give me my tribute."

The fat man got down ponderously, marched over to Eric and, to Rincewind's extreme surprise, groveled.

Rincewind felt something claw its way up his back and onto his shoulder, where a voice like a sheet of metal being torn in half said, "That's better. Very wossname, comfy. If you try and knock me off, demon, you can wossname your ear goodbye. What a turn up for the scrolls, eh? They seemed to be expecting him."

"Why do you keep saying wossname?" said Rincewind.

"Limited wossname. Doodah. Thingy. You know. It's got words in it," said the parrot.

"Dictionary?" said Rincewind. The passengers in the other chariots had got out and were also groveling to Eric, who was beaming like an idiot.

The parrot considered this.

"Yeah, probably," it said. "I've got to wing it to

you," it went on. "I thought you were a bit of a wossname at the start, but you seem to be delivering the wossname."

"Demon?" said Eric, airily.

"Yes?"

"What are they saying? Can't you speak their language?"

"Er, no," said Rincewind. "I can read it, though," he called out, as Eric turned away. "If you could just sort of make signs for them to write it down . . ."

It was around noon. In the jungle behind Rincewind creatures whooped and gibbered. Mosquitoes the size of hummingbirds whined around his head.

"Of course," he said, for the tenth time, "They've never really got around to inventing paper."

The stonemason stood back, handed the latest blunted obsidian chisel to his assistant, and gave Rincewind an expectant look.

Rincewind stood back and examined the rock critically.

"It's very good," he said. "I mean, it's a very good likeness. You've got his hairstyle and everything. Of course, he's not as, er, *square* as that normally but, yes, very good. And here's the chariot and there's the step-pyramids. Yes. Well, it looks as though they want you to go to the city with them," he said to Eric.

"Tell them yes," said Eric firmly.

Rincewind turned to the headman.

"Yes," he said.

"*¿[Hunched-figure-in-triple-feathered-headdress-over-three-dots]?*"

Rincewind sighed. Without saying a word, the stonemason put a fresh stone chisel into his unresisting fingers and manhandled a new slab of granite into position.

One of the problems of being a Tezuman, apart from having a god like Quezovercoatl, is that if you unexpectedly need to order an extra pint of milk tomorrow you probably should have started writing the note for the milkman last month. Tezumen are the only people who beat themselves to death with their own suicide notes.

It was late afternoon by the time the chariot trotted into the slab city around the largest pyramid, between lines of cheering Tezumen.

"This is more like it," said Eric, graciously acknowledging the cheers. "They're very pleased to see us."

"Yes," said Rincewind, gloomily. "I wonder why?"

"Well, because I'm the new ruler, of course."

"Hmm." Rincewind glanced sidelong at the parrot, who had been unnaturally silent for some time and was now cowering up against his ear like an elderly spinster in a strip club. It was having serious thoughts about the exquisite feather headdresses.

"Wossname bastards," it croaked. "Any wossname lays a hand on me and that wossname is minus one finger, I'm telling you."

"There's something not right about this," said Rincewind.

"What's that?" said the parrot.

"Everything."

"I'm telling you, one feather out of place—"

Rincewind wasn't used to people being pleased to see him. It was unnatural, and boded no good. These people were not only cheering, they were throwing flowers and hats. The hats were made out of stone, but the thought was there.

Rincewind thought they were rather odd hats.

They didn't have crowns. They were, in fact, mere discs with holes in the middle.

The procession trotted up the wide avenues of the city to a cluster of buildings at the foot of the pyramid, where another group of civic dignitaries was waiting for them.

They were wearing lots of jewelry. It was all basically the same. There are quite a lot of uses to which you can put a stone disc with a hole in the middle, and the Tezumen had explored all but one of them.

More important, though, were the boxes and boxes of treasure stacked in front of them. They were stuffed with jewels.

Eric's eyes widened.

"The tribute!" he said.

Rincewind gave up. It really was working. He didn't know how, he didn't know why, but at last it was all going Right. The setting sun glinted off a dozen fortunes. Of *course*, it belonged to Eric, presumably, but maybe there was enough for him, too . . .

"Naturally," he said weakly. "What else did you expect?"

* * *

And there was feasting, and long speeches that Rincewind couldn't understand but which were punctuated with cheers and nods and bows in Eric's direction. And there were long recitals of Tezuman music, which sounds like someone clearing a particularly difficult nostril.

Rincewind left Eric sitting proudly enthroned in the firelight and wandered disconsolately across to the pyramid.

"I was enjoying the wossname," said the parrot reproachfully.

"I can't settle down," said Rincewind. "I'm sorry, but this sort of thing has never happened to me before. All the jewels and things. Everything going as expected. It's not right."

He looked up the monstrous face of the steep pyramid, red and flickering in the firelight. Every huge block was carved with a bas-relief of Tezumen doing terribly inventive things to their enemies. It suggested that the Tezumen, whatever sterling qualities they possessed, were not traditionally inclined to welcome perfect strangers and heap them with jewels. The overall effect of the great heap of carvings was very artistic—it was just the details that were horrible.

61

While working his way along the wall he came to a huge door, which artistically portrayed a group of prisoners apparently being given a complete medical check-up.*

It opened into a short, torch-lit tunnel. Rincewind took a few steps along it, telling himself he could always hurry out again, and came out into a lofty space which occupied most of the inside of the pyramid.

There were more torches all around the walls, which illuminated everything quite well.

That wasn't really welcome because what they mainly illuminated was a giant-sized statue of Quezovercoatl, the Feathered Boa.

If you had to be in a room with that statue, you'd prefer it to be pitch dark.

Or, then again, perhaps not. A better option would be to put the thing in a darkened room while you had insomnia a thousand miles away, trying to forget what it looked like.

It's just a statue, Rincewind told himself. It's not real. They've just used their imagination, that's all.

"What the wossname is it?" said the parrot.

---

*From a distance it did, anyway. Close to, no.

"It's their god."

"Get away?"

"No, really. It's Quezovercoatl. Half man, half chicken, half jaguar, half serpent, half scorpion and half mad."

The parrot's beak moved as it worked this out.

"That makes a wossname total of three homicidal maniacs," it said.

"About right, yes," said the statue.

"*On the other hand*," said Rincewind instantly, "I do think it's frightfully important for people to have the right to worship in their own special way, and now I think we'll just be going, so just—"

"Please don't leave me here," said the statue. "Please take me with you."

"Could be tricky, could be tricky," Rincewind said hurriedly, backing away. "It's not me, you understand, it's just that where I come from everyone has this racial prejudice thing against thirty-foot-high people with fangs and talons and necklaces of skulls all over them. I just think you'll have trouble fitting in."

The parrot tweaked his ear. "It's coming from *behind* the statue, you stupid wossname," it croaked.

It turned out to be coming from a hole in the floor. A pale face peered shortsightedly up at Rincewind from the depths of a pit. It was an elderly, good-natured face with a faintly worried expression.

"Hallo?" said Rincewind.

"You don't know what it means to hear a friendly voice again," said the face, breaking into a grin. "If you could just sort of help me up . . . ?"

"Sorry?" said Rincewind. "You're a prisoner, are you?"

"Alas, this is so."

"I don't know that I ought to go around rescuing prisoners just like that," said Rincewind. "I mean, you might have done *anything*."

"I am entirely innocent of all crimes, I assure you."

"Ah, well, so you say," said Rincewind gravely. "But if the Tezumen have judged—"

"Wossname, wossname, *wossname*!" shrieked the parrot in his ear as it bounced up and down on his shoulder. "Haven't you got the faintest? Where've you been? He's a prisoner! A prisoner in a temple! You've got to rescue prisoners in temples! That's what they're bloody there for!"

"No it isn't," snapped Rincewind. "That's all you know! He's probably here to be sacrificed! Isn't that right?" He looked at the prisoner for confirmation.

The face nodded. "Indeed, you are correct. Flayed alive, in fact."

"There!" said Rincewind to the parrot. "See? You think you know everything! He's here to be flayed alive."

"Every inch of skin removed to the accompaniment of exquisite pain," added the prisoner, helpfully.

Rincewind paused. He thought he knew the meaning of the word "exquisite," and it didn't seem to belong anywhere near "pain."

"What, every bit?" he said.

"This is apparently the case."

"Gosh. What was it you did?"

The prisoner sighed. "You'd never believe me . . ." he said.

The Demon King let the mirror darken and drummed his fingers on his desk for a moment. Then he picked up a speaking tube and blew into it.

Eventually a distant voice said: "Yes, guv?"

"Yes *sir*!" snapped the King.

The distant voice muttered something. "Yes, SIR?" it added.

"Do we have a Quezovercoatl working here?"

"I'll see, guv." The voice faded, came back. "Yes, guv."

"Is he a Duke, Earl, Count or Baron?" said the King.

"No, guv."

"Well, what is he?"

There was a long silence at the other end.

"Well?" said the King.

"He's no one much, guv."

The King glared at the tube for some time. You try, he thought. You make proper plans, you try to get organized, you try to *help* people, and this is what you get.

"*Send him to see me,*" he said.

Outside, the music rose to a crescendo and stopped. The fires crackled. From the distant jungles a thousand glowing eyes watched the proceedings.

The high priest stood up and made a speech. Eric beamed like a pumpkin. A long line of Tezumen brought baskets of jewels which they scattered before him.

Then the high priest made a second speech. This one seemed to end on a question.

"Fine," said Eric. "Jolly good. Keep it up." He scratched his ear and ventured, "You can all have a half holiday."

The high priest repeated the question again, in a slightly impatient tone of voice.

"I'm the one, yes," said Eric, just in case they were unclear. "You've got it exactly right."

The high priest spoke again. This time there was no slightly about it.

"Let's just run through this again, shall we?" said the Demon King. He leaned back in his throne.

"You happened to find the Tezumen one day and decided, I think I recall your words correctly, that they were 'a bunch of Stone-Age no-hopers sitting around in a swamp being no trouble to anyone,' am I right? Whereupon you entered the mind of one of their high priests—I believe at that time they worshipped a small stick—drove him insane and inspired the tribes to unite, terrorize their neighbors and bring forth upon the continent a new nation dedicated to the proposition that all men should be taken to the top of ceremonial pyramids and be chopped up with stone knives." The King pulled his notes toward him. "Oh yes, some of them were also to be flayed alive," he added.

Quezovercoatl shuffled his feet.

"Whereupon," said the King, "they immediately engaged in a prolonged war with just about everyone else, bringing death and destruction to thousands of moderately blameless people, ekcetra, ekcetra. *Now, look, this sort of thing has got to stop.*"

Quezovercoatl swayed back a bit.

"It was only, you know, a hobby," said the imp. "I thought, you know, it was the right thing, sort of thing. Death and destruction and that."

"You did, did you?" said the King. "Thousands of more-or-less innocent people dying? Straight out of our hands," he snapped his fingers, "just like that. Straight off to their happy hunting ground or whatever. That's the trouble with you people. You don't think of the Big Picture. I mean, look at the Tezumen. Gloomy, unimaginative, obsessive . . . by now they could have invented a whole bureaucracy and taxation system that could have turned the minds of the continent to slag. Instead of which, they're just a bunch of second-rate axe-murderers. What a waste."

Quezovercoatl squirmed.

The King swiveled the throne back and forth a bit.

"Now, I want you to go straight back down there and tell them you're sorry," he said.

"Pardon?"

"Tell them you've changed your mind. Tell them that what you *really* wanted them to do was strive day and night to improve the lot of their fellow men. It'll be a winner."

"What?" said Quezovercoatl, looking extremely shifty. "You want me to manifest myself?"

"They've seen you already, haven't they? I saw the statue, it's very lifelike."

"Well, *yes*. I've appeared in dreams and that," said the demon uncertainly.

"Right, then. Get on with it."

Quezovercoatl was clearly unhappy about something.

"Er," he said. "You want me to actually materialize, sort of thing? I mean, actually sort of turn up on the spot?"

69

"Yes!"

"Oh."

The prisoner dusted himself down and extended a wrinkled hand to Rincewind.

"Many thanks. Ponce da Quirm," he said.

"Pardon?"

"It's my name."

"Oh."

"It's a proud old name," said da Quirm, searching Rincewind's eyes for any traces of mockery.

"Fine," said Rincewind blankly.

"We were searching for the Fountain of Youth," da Quirm went on.

Rincewind looked him up and down.

"Any luck?" he said politely.

"Not significantly, no."

Rincewind peered back down into the pit.

"You said *we*," he said. "Where's everyone else?"

"They got religion."

Rincewind looked up at the statue of Quezovercoatl. It took no imagination whatsoever to imagine what kind.

"I think," he said carefully, "that we had better go."

"Too true," said the old man. "And quickly, too. Before the Ruler of the World turns up."

Rincewind went cold. It starts, he thought. I knew it was all going to turn out badly, and this is where it starts. I must have an instinct for these things.

"How do you know about that?" he said.

"Oh, they've got this prophecy. Well, not a prophecy, really, it's more the entire history of the world, start to finish. It's written all over this pyramid," said da Quirm, cheerfully. "My word, I wouldn't like to be the Ruler when he arrives. They've got *plans*."

Eric stood up.

"Now just you listen to me," he said. "I'm not going to stand for this sort of thing. I'm your ruler, you know . . ."

Rincewind stared at the blocks nearest the statue. It had taken the Tezumen two stories, twenty years and ten thousand tons of granite to explain what they intended to do to the Ruler of the World, but the result was, well, graphic. He would be left in no doubt that they were annoyed. He might even go so far as to deduce that they were quite vexed.

"But why do they give him all these jewels to start with?" he said, pointing.

"Well, he *is* the Ruler," said da Quirm. "He's entitled to some respect, I suppose."

Rincewind nodded. There was a sort of justice in it. If you were a tribe who lived in a swamp in the middle of a damp forest, didn't have any metal, had been saddled with a god like Quezovercoatl, and then found someone who said he was in charge of the whole affair, you probably *would* want to spend some time explaining to him how incredibly disappointed you were. The Tezumen had never seen any reason to be subtle in dealing with deities.

It was a very good likeness of Eric.

His eye followed the story onto the next wall.

This block showed a very good likeness of Rincewind. He had a parrot on his shoulder.

"Hang on," he said. "That's me!"

"You should see what they're doing to you on

the next block," said the parrot smugly. "It'll turn your wossname."

Rincewind looked at the block. His wossname revolved.

"We'll just leave very quietly," he said firmly. "I mean, we won't stop to thank them for the meal. We can always send them a letter later. You know, so's not to be impolite."

"Just a moment," said da Quirm, as Rincewind dragged at his arm, "I haven't had a chance to read all the blocks yet. I want to see how the world's going to end—"

"How it's going to end for everyone else I don't know," said Rincewind grimly, dragging him down the tunnel. "I know how it's going to end for *me*."

He stepped out into the dawn light, which was fine. Where he went wrong was stepping into a semicircle of Tezumen. They had spears. They had exquisitely chipped obsidian spearheads, which, like their swords, were nowhere near as sophisticated as ordinary, coarse, inferior steel weapons. Was it better to know that you were going to be skewered by delicate examples of genuine ethnic origin rather than nasty forge-made items hammered out by people not in contact with the cycles of nature?

Probably not, Rincewind decided.

"I always say," said da Quirm, "that there is a good side to everything."

Rincewind, trussed to the next slab, turned his head with difficulty.

"Where is it at the moment, precisely?" he said.

Da Quirm squinted down across the swamps and the forest roof.

"Well. It's a first-class view from up here, to begin with."

"Oh, good," said Rincewind. "You know, I never would have looked at it like that. You're absolutely right. It's the kind of view you'll remember for the rest of your life, I expect. I mean, it's not as if it will be any great feat of recollection."

"There's no need to be sarcastic. I was only passing a remark."

"I want my mum," said Eric, from the middle slab.

"Chin up, lad," said da Quirm. "At least you're being sacrificed for something worthwhile. I just suggested they try using the wheels upright, so they'd roll. I'm afraid they're not very responsive to new ideas around here. Still, *nil desperandum*. Where there's life there's hope."

Rincewind growled. If there was one thing he couldn't stand, it was people who were fearless in the face of death. It seemed to strike at something absolutely fundamental in him.

"In fact," said da Quirm, "I think—" He rolled from side to side experimentally, tugging at the vines which were holding him down. "Yes, I think when they did these ropes up—yes, definitely, they—"

"What? What?" said Rincewind.

"Yes, definitely," said da Quirm. "I'm absolutely sure about it. They did them up very tightly and professionally. Not an inch of give in them anywhere."

"Thank you," said Rincewind.

The flat top of the truncated pyramid was in fact quite large, with plenty of room for statues, priests, slabs, gutters, knife-chipping production lines and all the other things the Tezumen needed for the bulk disposal of religion. In front of Rincewind several priests were busily chanting a long list of complaints about swamps, mosquitoes, lack of metal ore, volcanoes, the weather, the way obsidian never kept its edge, the trouble with having a god like Quezovercoatl, the way wheels never worked properly however often you laid them flat and pushed them, and so on.

The prayers of most religions generally praise and thank the gods involved, either out of general piety or in the hope that he or she will take the hint and start acting responsibly. The Tezumen, having taken a long hard look around their world and decided bluntly that things were just about as bad as they were ever going to get, had perfected the art of the plain-chant winge.

"Won't be long now," said the parrot, from its perch atop a statue of one of the Tezumen's lesser gods.

It had got there by a complicated sequence of events that had involved a lot of squawking, a cloud of feathers and three Tezuman priests with badly swollen thumbs.

"The high priest is just performing a wossname in honor of Quezovercoatl," it went on, conversationally. "You've drawn quite a crowd."

"I suppose you wouldn't kind of hop down here and bite through these ropes, would you?" said Rincewind.

"Not a chance."

"Thought so."

"Sun's coming up soon," the parrot continued. Rincewind felt that it sounded unnecessarily cheerful.

"I'm going to complain about this, demon," moaned Eric. "You wait till my mother finds out. My parents have got influence, you know."

"Oh, good," said Rincewind weakly. "Why don't you tell the high priest that if he cuts your heart out she'll be right down to the school tomorrow to complain."

The Tezuman priests bowed toward the sun, and all eyes in the crowd below turned to the jungle.

Where something was happening. There was the sound of crackling undergrowth. Tropical birds erupted through the trees, shrieking.

Rincewind, of course, could not see this.

"You never should have wanted to be ruler of the world," he said. "I mean, what did you expect? You can't expect people to be happy about seeing you. No one ever is when the landlord turns up."

"But they're going to kill me!"

"It's just their way of saying that, metaphorically, they're fed up with waiting for you to repaint the place and see to the drains."

The whole jungle was in an uproar now. Animals exploded out of the bushes as if running from a fire. A few heavy thumps indicated that trees were falling over.

At last a frantic jaguar crashed through the undergrowth and loped down the causeway. The Luggage was a few feet behind it.

It was covered with creepers, leaves and the feathers of various rare jungle fowls, some of which were now even rarer. The jaguar could have avoided it by zigging or zagging to either side, but sheer idiot terror prevented it. It made the mistake of turning its head to see what was behind.

This was the last mistake it ever made.

"You know that box of yours?" said the parrot.

"What about it?" said Rincewind.

"It's heading this way."

The priests peered down at the running figure far below. The Luggage had a straightforward way of dealing with things between it and its intended destination: it ignored them.

It was at this moment, against all his instincts, in great trepidation and, most unfortunately of all, in deep ignorance of what was happening, that Quezovercoatl himself chose to materialize on top of the pyramid.

Several of the priests noticed him. The knives fell from their fingers.

"Er," squeaked the demon.

Other priests turned around.

"Right. Now, I want you all to pay attention," squeaked Quezovercoatl, cupping his tiny hands around his main mouth in an effort to be heard.

This was very embarrassing. He'd enjoyed being the Tezuman god, he'd been really impressed by their single-minded devotion to duty, he'd been very gratified by the incredible lifelike statue in the pyramid, and it really hurt to have to reveal that, in one important particular, it was incorrect.

He was six inches high.

"Now then," he began, "this is very important—"

Unfortunately, no one ever found out why. At that moment the Luggage breasted the top of the

79

pyramid, its legs whirring like propellers, and landed squarely on the slabs.

There was a brief, flat squeak.

It was a funny old world, said da Quirm. You had to laugh, really. If you didn't, you'd go mad, wouldn't you? One minute strapped to a slab and about to undergo exquisite torture, the next being given breakfast, a change of clothes, a hot tub and a free lift out of the kingdom. It made you believe there was a god. Of course, the Tezumen *knew* there was a god, and that he was currently a small and distressing greasy patch on top of the pyramid. Which left them with a bit of a problem.

The Luggage squatted in the city's main plaza. The entire priesthood was sitting around it and watching it carefully, in case it did anything amusing or religious.

"Are you going to leave it behind?" said Eric.

"It's not as simple as that," said Rincewind. "It generally catches up. Let's just go away quickly."

"But we'll take the tribute, won't we?"

"I think that could be an amazingly bad idea," said Rincewind. "Let's just quietly go, while they're in a good temper. The novelty will wear off soon, I expect."

"And I've got to get on with my search for the Fountain of Youth," said da Quirm.

"Oh, yes," said Rincewind.

"I've devoted my whole life to it, you know," said the old man proudly.

Rincewind looked him up and down. "Really?" he said.

"Oh, yes. Exclusively. Ever since I was a boy."

Rincewind's expression was one of acute puzzlement.

"In that case," he began, in the manner of one talking to a child, "wouldn't it have been better . . . you know, more sensible . . . if you'd just got on with . . ."

"What?" said da Quirm.

"Oh, never mind," said Rincewind. "I'll tell you what, though," he added, "I think, in order to prevent you getting, you know, *bored*, we should present you with this wonderful talking parrot." He made a swift grab, while keeping his thumbs firmly out of harm's way. "It's a jungle fowl," he said. "Cruel to subject it to city life, isn't it?"

"I was born in a cage, you raving wossname!" screamed the parrot. Rincewind faced it, nose to beak.

"It's that or fricassee time," he said. The parrot opened its beak to bite his nose, saw his expression, and thought better of it.

"Polly want a biscuit," it managed, adding, *sotto voce, "wossnamewossnamewossname."*

"A dear little bird of my very own," said da Quirm. "I shall look after it."

"wossnamewossname."

They reached the jungle. A few minutes later the Luggage trotted after them.

It was noon in the kingdom of Tezuma.

From inside the main pyramid came the sounds of a very large statue being dismantled.

The priests sat around thoughtfully. Occasionally one of them stood up and made a short speech.

It was clear that points were being made. For example, how the economics of the kingdom depended on a buoyant obsidian knife industry, how the enslaved neighboring kingdoms had come to rely on the smack of firm government, and incidentally on the hack, slash and disemboweling of firm government as well, and on the terrible fate that awaited any people who didn't have gods. Godless people might get up to *anything*, they might turn against the fine old traditions of thrift and non-self-sacrifice that had made the kingdom what it was today, they might start wondering why, if they didn't have a god, they needed all these priests, *anything*.

The point was well put by Mazuma, the high priest, when he said: *"[Squashed-figure-with-broken-nose, jaguar claw, three feathers, stylized spiny anteater]."*

After a while a vote was taken.

By nightfall, the kingdom's leading stonemasons were at work on a new statue.

It was basically oblong, with lots of legs.

The Demon King drummed his fingers on his desk. It wasn't that he was unhappy about the fate of Quezovercoatl, who would now have to spend several centuries in one of the nether hells while he grew a new corporeal body. Serve him right, the ghastly little imp. Nor was it the broad trend of events on the pyramid. After all, the whole point of the wish business was to see to it that what the client got was exactly what he asked for and exactly what he didn't really want.

It was just that he didn't feel in control of things.

Which was of course ridiculous. If the best came to the best he could always materialize and sort things out personally. But he liked people to believe that all the bad things happening to them were just fate and destiny. It was one of the few things that cheered him up.

He turned back to the mirror. After a while he had to adjust the temporal control.

One minute the breathless, humid jungles of Klatch, the next . . .

"I thought we were going to go back to my room," Eric complained.

"I thought that, too," said Rincewind, shouting to be heard over the rumbling.

"Snap your fingers again, demon."

"Not on your life! There's plenty of places worse than this!"

"But it's all hot and dark."

Rincewind had to concede that. It was also shaking and noisy. When his eyes grew used to the blackness he could make out a few spots of light here and there, whose dim radiance suggested that they were inside something like a boat. There was a definite feel of carpentry about everything, and a powerful smell of wood shavings and glue. If it was a boat, then it was having an awfully painful launching down a slipway greased with rocks.

A jolt slung him heavily against a bulkhead.

"I must say," complained Eric, "if this is where the most beautiful woman in the world lives I don't think much of her choice of boodwah. You'd think she'd put a few cushions or something around the place."

"Boodwah?" said Rincewind.

"She's bound to have one," said Eric smugly. "I've read about 'em. She reclines on it."

"Tell me," said Rincewind, "have you ever felt the need to have a cold bath and a brisk run around the playing fields?"

"Never."

"It could be worth a try."

The rumbling stopped abruptly.

There was a distant clanging noise, such as might be made by a pair of great big gates being shut. Rincewind thought he heard some voices fading into the distance, and a chuckle. It wasn't a particularly pleasant chuckle, it was more of a snigger, and it boded no good for someone. Rincewind had a pretty good idea who.

He'd stopped wondering how he'd come to be here, wherever it was. Malign forces, that was probably it. At least nothing particularly dreadful was happening to him right now. Probably it was only a matter of time.

He groped around a bit until his fingers encountered what turned out to be, following an inspection by the light of the nearest knot-hole, a rope ladder. Further probing at one end of the hull, or whatever it was, brought him in contact with a small, round hatchway. It was bolted on the inside.

He crawled back to Eric.

"There's a door," he whispered.

"Where does it go?"

"It stays where it is, I think," said Rincewind.

"Find out where it leads to, demon!"

"Could be a bad idea," said Rincewind cautiously.

"Get on with it!"

Rincewind crawled gloomily to the hatch and grasped the bolt.

~~FAUST~~ ERIC

The hatch creaked open.

Down below—quite a long way below—there were damp cobblestones, across which a breeze was driving a few shreds of morning mist. With a little sigh, Rincewind unrolled the ladder.

Two minutes later they were standing in the gloom of what appeared to be a large plaza. A few buildings showed through the mist.

"Where are we?" said Eric.

"Search me."

"You don't *know*?"

"Not a clue," said Rincewind.

Eric glared at the mist-shrouded architecture. "Fat chance of finding the most beautiful woman in the world in a dump like this," he said.

It occurred to Rincewind to see what they had just climbed out of. He looked up.

Above them—a long way above them—and supported on four massive legs, which ran down to a huge wheeled platform, there was undoubtedly a huge wooden horse. More correctly, the rear of a huge wooden horse.

The builder could have put the exit hatch in a more dignified place, but for humorous reasons of his own had apparently decided not to.

"Er," said Rincewind.

Someone coughed.

He looked down.

The evaporating mists now revealed a broad circle of armed men, many of them grinning and all of them carrying mass-produced, soulless but above all *sharp* long spears.

"Ah," said Rincewind.

He looked back up at the hatchway. It said it all, really.

"The only thing I don't understand," said the captain of the guard, "is: why two of you? We were expecting maybe a hundred."

He leaned back on his stool, his great plumed helmet in his lap, a pleased smile on his face.

"Honestly, you Ephebians!" he said. "Talk about laugh! You must think we was born yesterday! All night nothing but sawing and hammering, the next thing there's a damn great wooden horse outside the gates, so I think, that's funny, a bloody great wooden horse with *airholes*. That's the kind of little detail I notice, see. *Airholes*. So I muster all the lads and we nips out extra early and drag it in the gates, as per expectations, and then we bides quiet, like, around it, waiting to see what it coughs up. In a manner of speaking. *Now*," he pushed his unshaven face close to Rincewind, "you've got a choice, see? Top seat or bottom seat, it's up to you. I just have to put the word in. You play discus with me and I'll play discus with you."*

"What seat?" said Rincewind, reeling from the gusts of garlic.

"It's the war triremes," said the sergeant cheerfully. "Three seats, see, one above the other? *Triremes*. You get chained to the oars for years, see, and it's all according whether you're in the top seat, up in the fresh air and that, or the bottom seat where"—he grinned— "you're not. So it's down to you, lads. Be cooperative and all you'll need to worry about will be the seagulls. *Now*. Why only the two of you?"

He leaned back again.

"Excuse me," said Eric, "is that Tsort, by any chance?"

"You wouldn't be trying to make fun of me, would you now, boy? Only there's such a thing as quinquiremes, see? You wouldn't like that at *all*."

---

*Ball games were unknown in the Discworld at this time.

"No, *sir*," said Eric. "If you please, sir, I'm just a little lad led astray by bad companionship."

"Oh, *thank* you," said Rincewind bitterly. "You just accidentally drew a lot of occult circles, did you, and—"

"Sarge! Sarge!" A soldier burst into the guard-room. The sergeant looked up.

"There's another of 'em, sarge! Right outside the gates this time!"

The sergeant grinned triumphantly at Rincewind.

"Oh, that's it, is it?" he said. "You were just the advance party, come to open the gates or whatever. *Right*. We'll just go and sort your friends out, and we'll be right back." He indicated the captives. "You stay here. If they move, do something horrible to them."

Rincewind and Eric were left alone with the guard.

"You know what you've done, don't you," said Eric. "You've only taken us all the way back to the Tsortean Wars! Thousands of years! We did it at school, the wooden horse, everything! How the beautiful Elenor was kidnaped from the Ephebians—or maybe it was by the Ephebians—

and there was this siege to get her back and everything." He paused. "Hey, that means I'm going to meet *her*." He paused again. "Wow!" he said.

Rincewind looked around the room. It didn't *look* ancient, but then it wouldn't, because it wasn't, yet. Everywhere in time was now, once you were there, or then. He tried to remember what little he knew of classical history, but it was just a confusion of battles, one-eyed giants and women launching thousands of ships with their faces.

"Don't you see?" hissed Eric, his glasses aglow. "They must have brought the horse in before the soldiers had hidden in it! We know what's going to happen! We could make a fortune!"

"How, exactly?"

"Well . . ." The boy hesitated. "We could bet on horses, that sort of thing."

"Great idea," said Rincewind.

"Yes, and—"

"All we've got to do is escape, then find out if they have horse races here, and then really try hard to remember the names of the horses that won races in Tsort thousands of years ago."

They went back to looking glumly at the floor.

That was the thing about time travel. You were never ready for it. About the only thing he could hope for, Rincewind decided, was finding da Quirm's Fountain of Youth and managing to stay alive for a few thousand years so he'd be ready to kill his own grandfather, which was the only aspect of time travel that had ever remotely appealed to him. He had always felt that his ancestors had it coming to them.

Funny thing, though. He could remember the famous wooden horse, which had been used to trick a way into the fortified city. He didn't remember anything about there being two of them. There was something inevitable about the next thought that turned up.

"Excuse me," he said to the guard. "This, er, this second wooden thing outside the gate . . . it's probably not a horse, I expect?"

"Well, of course you'd know that, wouldn't you?" said the guard. "You're spies."

"I bet it's more oblong and sort of smaller?" said Rincewind, his face a picture of innocent inquiry.

"You bet. Pretty unimaginative bastards, aren't you?"

"I *see.*" Rincewind folded his hands on his lap.

"Try to escape," said the guard. "Go on, just try it. You try it and see what happens."

"I expect your colleagues will be bringing it into the city," Rincewind went on.

"They might do that," the guard conceded.

Eric began to giggle.

It had begun to dawn on the guard that there was a lot of shouting going on in the distance. Someone tried to blow a bugle, but the notes gurgled into silence after a few bars.

"Bit of a fight going on out there, by the sound of it," said Rincewind. "People winning their spurs, doing heroic deeds of valor, being noticed by superior officers, that sort of thing. And here's you hanging around in here with us."

"I've got to stick to my post," said the guard.

"Exactly the right attitude," said Rincewind. "Never mind about everyone else out there fighting valiantly to defend their city and womenfolk against the foe. You stop in here and guard us. That's the spirit. They'll probably put up a statue to you in the city square, if there's one left. 'He did his duty,' they'll write on it."

The soldier appeared to think about this, and while he was doing so there was a terrible splintering creak from the direction of the main gates.

"Look," he said desperately, "if I just pop out for a moment . . ."

"Don't you worry about us," said Rincewind encouragingly. "It's not even as if we're armed."

"Right," said the soldier. "Thanks."

He gave Rincewind a worried smile and hurried off in the direction of the noise. Eric looked at Rincewind with something like admiration.

"That was actually quite amazing," he said.

"Going to go a long way, that lad," said Rincewind. "A sound military thinker if ever I saw one. Come on. Let's run away."

"Where to?"

Rincewind sighed. He'd tried to make his basic philosophy clear time and again, and people never got the message.

"Don't you worry about *to*," he said. "In my experience that always takes care of itself. The important word is *away*."

The captain raised his head cautiously over the barricade, and snarled.

"It's just a little box, sergeant," he snapped. "It's not even as if it could hold one or two men."

"Beg pardon, sir," said the sergeant, and his face was the face of a man whose world has changed a lot in a few short minutes. "It holds at least four, sir. Corporal Disuse and his squad, sir. I sent them out to open it, sir."

"Are you drunk, sergeant?"

"Not yet, sir," said the sergeant, with feeling.

"Little boxes don't eat people, sergeant."

"After that it got angry, sir. You can see what it did to the gates."

The captain peered over the broken timbers again.

"I suppose it grew legs and walked over there, did it?" he said sarcastically.

The sergeant broke into a relieved grin. At last they seemed to be on the same wavelength.

"Got it in one, sir," he said. "Legs. Hundreds of the little bleeders, sir."

The captain glared at him. The sergeant put on the poker face that has been handed down from NCO to NCO ever since one protoamphibian told another, lower-ranking protoamphibian to muster a squad of newts and Take That Beach. The captain was eighteen and fresh from the academy, where he had passed with flying colors in such subjects as Classical Tactics, Valedictory Odes and Military Grammar. The sergeant was fifty-five, and instead of an education he had spent about forty years attacking or being attacked by harpies, humans, cyclopses, furies and horrible things on legs. He felt put upon.

"Well, I'm going to have a look at it, sergeant—"

"—not a good plan, sir, if I may—"

"—and after I've had a look at it, sergeant, there is going to be trouble."

The sergeant threw him a salute. "Right you are, sir," he predicted.

The captain snorted and climbed over the barricade toward the box which sat, silent and unmoving, in its circle of devastation. The sergeant, meanwhile, slid into a sitting position behind the stoutest timber he could find and, with great determination, pulled his helmet down hard over his ears.

Rincewind crept through the streets of the city, with Eric tagging along behind.

"Are we going to find Elenor?" the boy said.

"No," said Rincewind firmly. "What we're going to do is, we're going to find another way out. And we're going to go out through it."

"That's not fair!"

"She's thousands of years older than you! I mean, attraction of the mature woman, all *right*, but it'd never work out."

"I demand that you take me to her," wailed Eric. "Avaunt!"

Rincewind stopped so sharply that Eric walked into him.

"Listen," he said. "We're in the middle of the most famously fatuous war there has ever been, any minute now thousands of warriors will be locked in mortal combat, and you want me to go and find this overrated female and say, my friend wants to know if you'll go out with him. Well, I won't." Rincewind stalked up to another gateway in the city wall; it was smaller than the main one, didn't have any guards, and had a wicket gate in it. Rincewind slid back the bolts.

"This isn't anything to do with us," he said. "We haven't even been born yet, we're not old enough to fight, it isn't our business and we're not going to do anything more to upset the course of history, all right?"

He opened the door, which saved the entire Ephebian army a bit of effort. They were just about to knock.

All day long the noise of battle raged. This was chronicled by later historians, who went on at length about beautiful women being kidnaped, fleets being assembled, wooden animals being constructed, heroes fighting one another, and completely failed to mention the part played by Rincewind, Eric and the Luggage. The Ephebians did notice, however, how enthusiastically the Tsortean soldiery ran toward them . . . not so much keen to get into battle as very anxious to get away from something else.

The historians also failed to note another interesting fact about ancient Klatchian warfare, which was that it was still at that stage quite primitive and just between soldiers and hadn't yet been thrown open to the general public. Basically, everyone knew that one side or the other would win, a few unlucky generals would get their heads chopped off, large sums of money would be paid in tribute to the winners, everyone would go home for the harvest and that bloody woman would have to make up her mind whose side she was on, the hussy.

So Tsortean street life went on more or less as normal, with the citizens stepping around the occasional knots of fighting men or trying to sell them kebabs. Several of the more enterprising ones began dismantling the wooden horse for souvenirs.

Rincewind didn't attempt to understand it. He sat down at a street café and watched a spirited battle take place between market stalls, so that amid the cries of "Ripe olives!" there were the screams of the wounded and shouts of "Mind your backs *please*, mêlée coming through."

The hard part was watching the soldiers apologize when they bumped into customers. The even harder part was getting the café owner to accept a coin bearing the head of someone whose great-great-great-grandfather wasn't born yet. Fortunately, Rincewind was able to persuade the man that the future was another country.

"And a lemonade for the boy," he added.

"My parents let me drink wine," said Eric. "I'm allowed one glass."

"I bet you are," said Rincewind.

The owner industriously swabbed the tabletop, spreading its coating of dregs and spilt retsina into a thin varnish.

"Up for the fight, are you?" he said.

"In a manner of speaking," said Rincewind guardedly.

"I shouldn't wander around too much," said the owner. "They do say a civilian let the Ephebians in—*not that I've got anything against Ephebians, a fine body of men*," he added hurriedly, as a knot of soldiery jogged past. "A stranger, they say. That's cheating, using civilians. There's people out looking for him so's they can explain." He made a chopping motion with his hand.

Rincewind stared at the hand as though hypnotized.

Eric opened his mouth. Eric screeched and clutched at his shins.

"Have they got a description?" Rincewind said.

"Don't think so."

"Well, best of luck to them," said Rincewind, rather more cheerfully.

"What's up with the lad?"

"Cramp."

When the man had gone back behind his counter Eric hissed, "You didn't have to go and kick me!"

"You're quite right. It was an entirely voluntary act on my part."

A heavy hand dropped onto Rincewind's shoulder. He looked around and up into the face of an Ephebian centurion. A soldier beside him said: "That's the one, sarge. I'd bet a year's salt."

"Who'd of thought it?" said the sergeant. He gave Rincewind an evil grin. "Up we come, chummy. The chief would like a word with you."

Some talk of Alexander and some of Hercules, of Hector and Lysander and such great names as these. In fact, throughout the history of the multiverse people have said nice things about every cauliflower-eared sword-swinger, at least in their vicinity, on the basis that it is a lot safer that way. It's funny how the people have always respected the kind of commander who comes up with strategies like "I want fifty thousand of you chappies to rush at the enemy," whereas the more thoughtful commanders who say things like "Why don't we build a damn great wooden horse and then nip in at the back gate while they're all around the thing waiting for us to come out" are considered only one step above common oiks and not the kind of person you'd lend money to.

This is because most of the first type of commander are brave men, whereas cowards make far better strategists.

Rincewind was dragged before the Ephebian leaders, who had set up a command post in the city's main square so that they could oversee the storming of the central citadel, which loomed over the city on its vertiginous hill. They were not too close, however, because the defenders were dropping rocks.

They were discussing strategy when Rincewind arrived. The consensus seemed to be that if really large numbers of men were sent to storm the mountain, then enough might survive the rocks to take the citadel. This is essentially the basis of all military thinking.

Several of the more impressively dressed chieftains glanced up when Rincewind and Eric approached, gave them a look which suggested that maggots were more interesting, and turned away again. The only person who seemed pleased to see them—

—didn't look like a soldier at all. He had the armor, which was tarnished, and he had the helmet, which looked as though its plume had been used as a paintbrush, but he was skinny and had all the military bearing of a weasel. There was something vaguely familiar about his face, though. Rincewind thought it looked quite handsome.

"Pleased to see them" was only a comparative description. He was the only one who acknowledged their existence.

He was lounging in a chair and feeding the Luggage with sandwiches.

"Oh, hallo," he said gloomily. "It's you."

It was amazing how much information can be crammed into a couple of words. To achieve the same effect the man could have said: It's been a long night, I'm having to organize everything from wooden horse building to the laundry rota, these idiots are about as much help as a rubber hammer, I never wanted to be here anyway and, on top of all this, there's you. Hallo, you.

He indicated the Luggage, which opened its lid expectantly.

"This yours?" he said.

"Sort of," said Rincewind guardedly. "I can't afford to pay for anything it's done, mind you."

"Funny little thing, isn't it?" said the soldier. "We found it herding fifty Tsorteans into a corner. Why was it doing that, do you think?"

Rincewind thought quickly. "It has this amazing ability to know when people are thinking about harming me," he said. He glared at the Luggage as one might glare at a sly, evil-tempered and generally reprehensible family pet who, after years of biting visitors, has rolled over on its scabby back and played at Lovable Puppy to impress the bailiffs.

"Yes?" said the man, without much surprise. "Magic, is it?"

"Yes."

"Something in the wood, is it?"

"Yes."

"Good job we didn't build the sodding horse out of it, then."

"Yes."

"Got into it by magic, did you?"

"Yes."

"Thought so." He threw another sandwich at the Luggage. "Where you from?"

Rincewind decided to come clean. "The future," he said. This didn't have the expected effect. The man just nodded.

"Oh," he said, and then he said, "Did we win?"

"Yes."

"Oh. I suppose you can't remember the results of any horse races?" said the man, without much hope.

"No."

"I thought you probably wouldn't. Why did you open the gate for us?"

It occurred to Rincewind that saying it was because he had always been a firm admirer of the Ephebian political position would not, strangely enough, be the right thing to do. He decided to try the truth again. It was a novel approach and worth experimenting with.

"I was looking for a way out," he said.

"To run away."

"Yes."

"Good man. Only sensible thing, in the circumstances." He noticed Eric, who was staring at the other captains clustered around their table and deep in argument.

"You, lad," he said. "Want to be a soldier when you grow up?"

"No, sir."

The man brightened a bit.

"That's the stuff," he said.

"I want to be a eunuch, sir," Eric added.

Rincewind's head turned as though it was being dragged.

"*Why?*" he said, and then came up with the obvious answer at the same time as Eric: "Because you get to work in a harem all day long," they chorused slowly.

The captain coughed.

"You're not this boy's teacher, are you?" he said.

"No."

"Do you think anyone has explained to him—?"

"No."

"Perhaps it would be a good idea if I got one of the centurions to have a word? You'd be amazed at the grasp of language those chaps have got."

"Do him the power of good, I expect," said Rincewind.

The soldier picked up his helmet, sighed, nodded

at the sergeant and smoothed out the creases in his cloak. It was a grubby cloak.

"I think I'm expected to tell you off, or something," he said.

"What for?"

"Spoiling the war, apparently."

"Spoiling the war?"

The soldier sighed. "Come on. Let's go for a stroll. Sergeant—you and a couple of lads, please."

A stone whistled down from the fort high above them, and shattered.

"They can hold out for bloody weeks, up there," said the soldier gloomily, as they walked away with the Luggage padding patiently behind them. "I'm Lavaeolus. Who're you?"

"He's my demon," said Eric.

Lavaeolus raised an eyebrow, the closest he ever came to expressing surprise at anything.

"Is he? I suppose it takes all sorts. Any good at getting in places, is he?"

"He's more the getting-out kind," said Eric.

"Right," said Lavaeolus. He stopped beside a building and walked up and down a bit with his hands in his pockets, tapping on the flagstones with the toe of his sandal.

107

"Just here, I think, sergeant," he said, after a while.

"Right you are, sir."

"Look at that lot, will you?" said Lavaeolus, while the sergeant and his men started to lever up the stones. "That bunch around the table. Brave lads, I'll grant you, but look at them. Too busy posing for triumphant statues and making sure the historians spell their names right. Bloody *years* we've been laying siege to this place. More *military*, they said. You know, they actually enjoy it? I mean, when all's said and done, who cares? Let's just get it over with and go home, that's what I say."

"Found it, sir," said the sergeant.

"Right." Lavaeolus didn't look around. "O-*kay*." He rubbed his hands together. "Let's sort this out, and then we can get an early night. Would you care to accompany me? Your pet might be useful."

"What are we going to do?" said Rincewind suspiciously.

"We're just going to meet some people."

"Is it dangerous?"

A stone smashed through the roof of a building nearby.

108

"No, not really," said Lavaeolus. "Compared to staying out here, I mean. And if the rest of them try to storm the place, you know, in a proper military way—"

The hole led into a tunnel. The tunnel, after winding a bit, led to stairs. Lavaeolus mooched along it, occasionally kicking bits of fallen masonry as if he had a personal grudge against them.

"Er," said Rincewind, "where does this lead?"

"Oh, it's just a secret passageway into the center of the citadel."

"You know, I thought it would be something like that," said Rincewind. "I've got an instinct for it, you know. And I expect all the really top Tsorteans will be up there, will they?"

"I hope so," said Lavaeolus, trudging up the steps.

"With lots of guards?"

"Dozens, I imagine."

"Highly trained, too?"

Lavaeolus nodded. "The best."

"And this is where we're going," said Rincewind, determined to explore the full horror of the plan as one probes the site of a rotting tooth.

"That's right."

"All six of us."

"And your box, of course."

"Oh, yes," said Rincewind, making a face in the darkness.

The sergeant tapped him gently on the shoulder and leaned forward.

"Don't you worry about the captain, sir," he said. "He's got the finest military brain on the continent."

"How do you know? Has anyone ever *seen* it?" said Rincewind.

"You see, sir, what it is, he likes to get it over with without anyone getting hurt, sir, especially him. That's why he dreams up things like the horse, sir. And bribing people and that. We got into civvies last night and come in and got drunk in a pub with one of the palace cleaners, see, and found out about this tunnel."

"Yes, but secret passages!" said Rincewind. "There'll be guards and everything at the other end!"

"No, sir. They use it to store the cleaning things, sir."

There was a clang in the darkness ahead of them. Lavaeolus had tripped over a mop.

"Sergeant?"

"Sir?"

"Just open the door, will you?"

Eric was tugging at Rincewind's robe.

"What?" said Rincewind testily.

"You know who Lavaeolus *is*, don't you?" whispered Eric.

"Well—"

"He's *Lavaeolus*!"

"Get away?"

"Don't you know the Classics?"

"That isn't one of these horse races we're supposed to remember, is it?"

Eric rolled his eyes. "Lavaeolus was responsible for the fall of Tsort, on account of being so cunning," he said. "And then afterward it took him ten years to get home and he had all sorts of adventures with temptresses and sirens and sensual witches."

"Well, I can see why you've been studying him. Ten years, eh? Where did he live?"

"About two hundred miles away," said Eric earnestly.

"Kept getting lost, did he?"

"And when he got home he fought his wife's

111

suitors and everything, and his dear old dog recognized him and died."

"Oh, dear."

"It was the carrying his slippers in its mouth for fifteen years that killed it off."

"Shame."

"And you know what, demon? All this *hasn't happened yet*. We could save him all that trouble!"

Rincewind thought about this. "We could tell him to get a better navigator, for a start," he said.

There was a creak. The soldiers had got the door open.

"Everyone fall in, or whatever the bloody stupid command is," said Lavaeolus. "The magic box to the front, please. No killing anyone unless it's really necessary. Try not to damage things. Right. Forward."

The door led into a column-lined corridor. There was the distant murmur of voices.

The troop crept toward the sound until it reached a heavy curtain. Lavaeolus took a deep breath, pushed it aside and stepped forward and launched into a prepared speech.

"Now, I want to make myself *absolutely* clear," he said. "I don't want there to be any unpleasantness of any kind, or any shouting for guards and so forth. Or indeed any shouting at all. We will just take the young lady and go home, which is where anyone of any sense ought to be. Otherwise I shall really have to put everyone to the sword, and I hate having to do things like that."

The audience to this statement did not appear to be impressed. This was because it was a small child on a potty.

Lavaeolus changed mental gear and went on smoothly: "On the other hand, if you don't tell me where everyone is, I shall ask the sergeant here to give you a really hard smack."

The child took its thumb out of its mouth. "Mummy is seeing to Cassie," it said. "Are you Mr. Beekle?"

"I don't think so," said Lavaeolus.

"Mr. Beekle is a silly." The child withdrew its thumb and, with the air of one concluding some exhaustive research, added: "Mr. Beekle is a poo."

"Sergeant?"

"Sir?"

"Guard this child."

"Yessir. Corporal?"

"Sarge?"

"Take care of the kid."

"Yes, sarge. Private Archeios?"

"Yes, corp," said the soldier, his voice gloomy with prescience.

"See to the sprog."

Private Archeios looked around. There were only Rincewind and Eric left and, while it was true that a civilian was in every respect the lowest possible rank there was, coming somewhere after the regimental donkey, the expressions on their faces suggested that they weren't about to take any orders.

Lavaeolus wandered across the room and listened at another curtain.

"We could tell him all kinds of stuff about his future," hissed Eric. "He had—I mean, he *will* have—all kinds of things happen to him. Shipwrecks and magic and all his crew turned into animals and stuff like that."

"Yes. We could say 'Walk home,'" said Rincewind.

The curtain swished aside.

There was a woman there—plump, good-looking in a slightly faded way, wearing a black dress and the beginnings of a mustache. A number of children of varying sizes were trying to hide behind her. Rincewind counted at least seven of them.

"Who's that?" said Eric.

"Ahem," said Rincewind. "I rather think it's Elenor of Tsort."

"Don't be silly," whispered Eric. "She looks like my mum. Elenor was much younger and was all—" His voice gave out and he made several wavy motions with his hand, indicative of the shape of a woman who would probably be unable to keep her balance.

Rincewind tried not to catch the sergeant's eye.

"Yes," he said, going a bit red. "Well, you see. Er. You're absolutely right, but well, it's been a long siege, hasn't it, what with one thing and another."

"I don't see what that's got to do with it," said Eric sternly. "The Classics never said anything about children. They said she spent all her time mooning around the towers of Tsort and pining for her lost love."

"Well, yes, I expect she did pine a *bit*," said Rincewind. "Only, you know, you can only pine so much, and it must have been a bit chilly up on those towers."

"You can catch your death, mooning," nodded the sergeant.

Lavaeolus watched the woman thoughtfully. Then he bowed.

"I expect you know why we're here, my lady?" he said.

"If you touch any of the children I shall scream," said Elenor flatly.

Once again Lavaeolus showed that along with his guerrilla abilities was a marked reluctance to waste a prepared speech once he had it all sorted out in his head.

"Fair maiden," he began. "We have faced many dangers in order to rescue you and take you back to your loved . . ." His voice faltered. ". . . ones. Er. This has all gone terribly wrong, hasn't it?"

"I can't help it," said Elenor. "The siege seemed to go on for such a long time and King Mausoleum was very kind and I never liked it much in Ephebe anyway—"

"Where is everyone now? The Tsorteans, I mean. Apart from you."

"They're all out on the battlements throwing rocks, if you must know."

Lavaeolus flung up his hands in desperation.

"Couldn't you, you know, have slipped us a note or something? Or invited us to one of the christenings?"

"You all seemed to be enjoying yourselves so much," she said.

Lavaeolus turned and shrugged gloomily. "All right," he said. "Fine. QED. No problem. I *wanted* to leave home and spend ten years sitting in a swamp with a bunch of meat-headed morons. It wasn't as if I had anything important to do back home, just a little kingdom to rule, that sort of thing. O-*kay*. Well, then. We might as well be off. I'm sure I don't know how I shall break it to everyone," he said bitterly, "they were having such fun. They'll probably have a bloody great banquet and laugh about it and get drunk, it'd be their style."

He looked at Rincewind and Eric.

"You might as well tell me what happens next," he said. "I'm sure you know."

"Um," said Rincewind.

"The city burns down," said Eric. "Especially

117

the topless towers. I didn't ˙get to see them," he added sulkily.

"Who did it? Their lot or our lot?" said Lavaeolus.

"Your lot, I think," said Eric.

Lavaeolus sighed. "Sounds like them," he said. He turned to Elenor. "Our lot—that is, my lot—are going to burn down the city," he said. "It sounds very heroic. It's just the kind of thing they go for. It might be a good idea to come with us. Bring the kids. Make it a day out for all the family, why don't you?"

Eric pulled Rincewind's ear toward his mouth.

"This is a joke, isn't it?" he said. "She's not really the fair Elenor, you're just having me on?"

"It's always the same with these hot-blooded types," said Rincewind. "They definitely go downhill at thirty-five."

"It's the pasta that does it," said the sergeant.

"But I read where she was the most beautiful—"

"Ah, well," said the sergeant. "If you're going to go around *reading*—"

"The thing is," said Rincewind quickly, "it's what they call dramatic necessity. No one's going to be interested in a war fought over a, a quite pleasant lady, moderately attractive in a good light. Are they?"

Eric was nearly in tears.

"But it said her face launched a thousand ships—"

"That's what you call metaphor," said Rincewind.

"Lying," the sergeant explained, kindly.

"Anyway, you shouldn't believe everything you read in the Classics," Rincewind added. "They never check their facts. They're just out to sell legends."

Lavaeolus, meanwhile, was deep in argument with Elenor.

"All right, all right," he said. "Stay here if you like. Why should I care? Come on, you lot. We're going. What are you doing, Private Archeios?"

"I'm being a horse, sir," explained the soldier.

"He's Mr. Poo," said the child, who was wearing Private Archeios' helmet.

"Well, when you've finished being a horse, find us an oil lamp. I caught my knees a right wallop in that tunnel."

*   *   *

Flames roared over Tsort. The entire hubward sky was red.

Rincewind and Eric watched from a rock down by the beach.

"They're not topless towers, anyway," said Eric after a while. "I can see the tops."

"I think they meant toppleless towers," Rincewind hazarded, as another one collapsed, red-hot, into the ruins of the city. "And that was wrong, too."

They watched in silence for a while longer, and then Eric said, "Funny, that. The way you tripped over the Luggage and dropped the lamp and everything."

"Yes," said Rincewind shortly.

"Makes you think history is always going to find a way to work itself out."

"Yes."

"Good, though, the way your Luggage rescued everyone."

"Yes."

"Funny to see all those kids riding on its back."

"Yes."

"Everyone seems quite pleased about it."

120

The opposing armies were, at any rate. No one was bothering to ask the civilians, whose views on warfare were never very reliable. Among the soldiery, at least among the soldiery of a certain rank, there was a lot of back-slapping and telling of anecdotes, jovial exchanging of shields and a general consensus that, what with fires and sieges and armadas and wooden horses and everything, it had been a jolly good war. The sound of singing echoed across the wine-dark sea.

"Hark at them," said Lavaeolus, emerging from the gloom around the beached Ephebian ships. "It'll be fifteen choruses of 'The Ball of Philodelphus' next, you mark my words. Lot of idiots with their brains in their jockstraps."

He sat down on the rock. "Bastards," he said, with feeling.

"Do you think Elenor will be able to explain it all to her boyfriend?" said Eric.

"I imagine so," said Lavaeolus. "They usually can."

"She did get married. And she's got lots of children," said Eric.

Lavaeolus shrugged. "A moment's wild passion," he said. He gave Rincewind a sharp look.

121

"Hey, you, demon," he said. "I'd like a quiet word, if I may."

He led Rincewind toward the boats, pacing heavily across the damp sand as if there was a lot weighing on his mind.

"I'm going home tonight, on the tide," he said. "No sense in hanging about here, what with the war being over and everything."

"Good idea."

"If there's one thing I hate, it's sea voyages," said Lavaeolus. He gave the nearest boat a kick. "It's all idiots striding around and shouting, you know? Pull this, lower that, avast the other. And I get sea-sick, too."

"It's heights with me," said Rincewind, sympathetically.

Lavaeolus kicked the boat again, obviously wrestling with some big emotional problem.

"The thing *is*," he said, wretchedly. "You wouldn't happen to know if I get home all right, would you?"

"What?"

"It's only a few hundred miles, it shouldn't take too long, should it?" said Lavaeolus, radiating anxiety like a lighthouse.

"Oh." Rincewind looked at the man's face. Ten years, he thought. And all kinds of weird stuff with winged wossnames and sea-monsters. On the other hand, would it do him any good to know?

"You get home okay," he said. "You're well-known for it, in fact. There's whole legends about you going home."

"Phew." Lavaeolus leaned against a hull, took off his helmet and wiped his forehead. "That's a load off my mind, I'll tell you. I was afraid the gods might have a grudge against me."

Rincewind said nothing.

"They get a bit angry if you go around thinking up ideas like wooden horses and tunnels," said Lavaeolus. "They're traditionalists, you know. They prefer people just to hack at one another. I thought, you see, that if I could show people how to get what they wanted more easily they'd stop being so bloody stupid."

From further along the shoreline came the sound of male voices raised in song:

"—vestal virgins, Came down from Heliodeliphilodelphiboschromenos, And when the ball was over, There were—"

"It never works," said Rincewind.

123

"It's got to be worth a try, though. Hasn't it?"

"Oh, yes."

Lavaeolus slapped him on the back. "Cheer up," he said. "Things can only get better."

They walked out into the dark breakers where Lavaeolus' ship was riding at anchor, and Rincewind watched him swim out and climb aboard. After a while the oars were shipped, or unshipped, or whatever they called it when they were stuck through the holes in the sides, and the boat moved slowly out into the bay.

A few voices floated back over the surf.

"Point the pointed end that way, sergeant."

"Aye aye, sir!"

"And don't *shout*. Did I tell you to shout? Why do you all have to shout? Now I'm going downstairs for a lie down."

Rincewind trudged back up the beach. "The trouble is," he said, "is that things *never* get better, they just stay the same, only more so. But he's going to have enough to worry about."

Behind him, Eric blew his nose.

"That was the saddest thing I've ever heard," he said.

From farther along the beach the Ephebian and Tsortean armies were still in full voice around their convivial campfires.

"—the village harpy she was there—"

"Come on," said Rincewind. "Let's go home."

"You know the funny thing about his name?" said Eric, as they strolled along the sand.

"No. What do you mean?"

"Lavaeolus means 'Rinser of winds.'"

Rincewind looked at him.

"He's my ancestor?" he said.

"Who knows?" said Eric.

"Oh. Gosh." Rincewind thought about this. "Well, I wish I'd told him to avoid getting married. Or visiting Ankh-Morpork."

"It probably isn't even built yet . . ."

Rincewind tried snapping his fingers.

This time it worked.

Astfgl sat back. He wondered what *did* happen to Lavaeolus.

Gods and demons, being creatures outside of time, don't move in it like bubbles in the stream. Everything happens at the same time for them.

125

This should mean that they know everything that is going to happen because, in a sense, it already has. The reason they don't is that reality is a big place with a lot of interesting things going on, and keeping track of all of them is like trying to use a very big video recorder with no freeze button or tape counter. It's usually easier just to wait and see.

One day he'd have to go and look.

Right here and now, insofar as the words can be employed about an area outside of space and time, matters were not progressing well. Eric seemed marginally more likeable, which wasn't acceptable. He also appeared to have changed the course of history, although this is impossible since the only thing you can do to the course of history is facilitate it.

What was needed was something climactic. Something really soul-destroying.

The Demon King realized he was twirling his mustaches.

The trouble with snapping your fingers is that you never knew what it would lead to . . .

Everything around Rincewind was black. It wasn't simply an absence of color. It was a darkness that flatly denied any possibility that color might ever have existed.

His feet weren't touching anything, and he appeared to be floating. There was something else missing. He couldn't quite put his finger on it.

"Are you there, Eric?" he ventured.

A clear voice nearby said: "Yes. Are you there, demon?"

"Ye—ess."

"Where are we? Are we falling?"

"I don't think so," said Rincewind, speaking from experience. "There's no rushing wind. You get a rushing wind when you're falling. Also your past life flashes before your eyes, and I haven't seen anything I recognize yet."

"Rincewind?"

"Yes?"

"When I open my mouth no sounds come out."

"Don't be—" Rincewind hesitated. He wasn't making any sound either. He knew what he was saying, it just wasn't reaching the outside world. But he could hear Eric. Perhaps the words just gave up on his ears and went straight to his brain.

"It's probably some kind of magic, or something," he said. "There's no air. That's why there's no sound. All the little bits of air sort of knock together, like marbles. That's how you get sound, you know."

"Is it? Gosh."

"So we're surrounded by absolutely nothing," said Rincewind. "Total nothing." He hesitated. "There's a word for it," he said. "It's what you get when there's nothing left and everything's been used up."

"Yes. I think it's called the bill," said Eric.

Rincewind gave this some thought. It sounded about right. "Okay," he said. "The bill. That's where we are. Floating in absolute bill. Total, complete, rock-hard bill."

Astfgl was going frantic now. He had spells that could find anyone anywhere, anywhen, and they weren't *anywhere*. One minute he was watching them on the beach, the next . . . nothing.

That left only two other places.

Fortunately he chose the wrong one first.

"Even some stars would be nice," said Eric.

"There's something very odd about all this," said Rincewind. "I mean, do you feel cold?"

"No."

"Well, do you feel warm?"

"No. I don't feel anything much, really."

"No hot, no cold, no light, no heat, no air," said Rincewind. "Just bill. How long have we been here?"

"Don't know. Seems like ages, but . . ."

"Aha. I'm not sure there's any time, either. Not what you'd call proper time. Just the kind of time people make up as they go along."

"Well, I didn't expect to see anyone else here," said a voice by Rincewind's ear.

It was a slightly put-upon voice, a voice made for complaining in, but at least there was no hint of menace. Rincewind let himself float around.

A little rat-faced man was sitting cross-legged, watching him with vague suspicion. He had a pencil behind one ear.

"Ah. Hallo," said Rincewind. "And where is here, exactly?"

"Nowhere. S'whole point, innit?"

"Nowhere at all?"

"Not yet."

"All right," said Eric. "When is it going to be somewhere?"

129

"Hard to say," said the little man. "Looking at the pair of you, and taking one thing with another, metabolic rates and that, I'd say that this place is due to become somewhere in, well, give or take a bit, in about five hundred seconds." He began to unwrap the pack in his lap. "Fancy a sandwich while we're waiting?"

"What? Would I—" At this point Rincewind's stomach, aware that if his brain was allowed to make the running it was in danger of losing the initiative, cut in and prompted him to say, "What sort?"

"Search me. What sort would you like it to be?"

"Sorry?"

"Don't mess about. Just say what sort you'd like it to be."

"Oh?" Rincewind stared at him. "Well, if you've got egg and cress—"

"Let there be egg and cress, sort of thing," said the little man. He reached into the package, and proffered a white triangle to Rincewind.

"Gosh," said Rincewind. "What a coincidence."

"It should be starting any minute now," said the little man. "Over—not that they've got any proper directions sorted out yet, of course, not them—there."

"All I can see is darkness," said Eric.

"No you can't," said the little man, triumphantly. "You're just seeing what there is before the darkness has been installed, sort of thing." He gave the not-yet-darkness a dirty look. "Come on," he said. "Why are we waiting, why-eye are we waiting?"

"Waiting for what?" said Rincewind.

"Everything."

"Everything what?" said Rincewind.

"Everything. Not everything what. Everything, sort of thing."

Astfgl peered around through the swirling gas clouds. At least he was in the right place. The whole point about the end of the universe was that you couldn't go past it accidentally.

The last few embers winked out. Time and space collided silently, and collapsed.

Astfgl coughed. It can get so very lonely, when you're twenty million light-years from home.

"Anyone there?" he said.

YES.

The voice was right by his ear. Even demon kings can shiver.

"Apart from you, I mean," he said. "Have you seen anybody?"

YES.

"Who?"

EVERYONE.

Astfgl sighed. "I mean anyone *recently*."

IT'S BEEN VERY QUIET, said Death.

"Damn."

WERE YOU EXPECTING SOMEONE ELSE?

"I thought there might be someone called Rincewind, but—" Astfgl began.

Death's eyesockets flared red. THE WIZARD? he said.

"No, he's a dem—" Astfgl stopped. For what would have been several seconds, had time still existed, he floated in a state of horrible suspicion.

"A *human*?" he growled.

IT IS STRETCHING THE TERM A LITTLE, BUT YOU ARE BROADLY CORRECT.

"Well, I'll be damned!" Astfgl said.

I BELIEVE YOU ALREADY ARE.

The Demon King extended a shaking hand. His

mounting fury was overriding his sense of style; his red silk gloves ripped as the talons unfolded.

And then, because it's never a good idea to get on the wrong side of anyone with a scythe, Astfgl said, "Sorry you've been troubled," and vanished. Only when he judged himself out of Death's extremely acute hearing did he scream his rage.

Nothingness uncoiled its interminable length through the drafty spaces at the end of time.

Death waited. After a while his skeletal fingers began to drum on the handle of his scythe.

Darkness lapped around him. There wasn't even any infinity anymore.

He attempted to whistle a few snatches of unpopular songs between his teeth, but the sound was simply sucked into nothingness.

Forever was over. All the sands had fallen. The great race between entropy and energy had been run, and the favorite had been the winner after all.

Perhaps he ought to sharpen the blade again?

No.

Not much point, really.

Great roils of absolutely nothing stretched into what would have been called the distance, if there had been a space-time reference frame to give words like "distance" any sensible meaning anymore.

There didn't seem to be much to *do*.

PERHAPS IT'S TIME TO CALL IT A DAY, he thought.

Death turned to go but, just as he did so, he heard the faintest of noises. It was to sound what one photon is to light, so weak and feeble that it would have passed entirely unheard in the din of an operating universe.

It was a tiny piece of matter, popping into existence.

Death stalked over to the point of arrival and watched carefully.

It was a paperclip.*

---

*Many people think it should have been a hydrogen molecule, but this is against the observed facts. Everyone who has found a hitherto unknown egg-whisk jamming an innocent kitchen drawer knows that raw matter is continually flowing into the universe in fairly developed forms, popping into existence normally in ashtrays, vases and glove compartments. It chooses its shape to allay suspicion, and common manifestations are paperclips, the pins out of shirt packaging, the little keys for central heating radiators, marbles, bits of crayon, mysterious sections of herb-chopping devices and old Kate Bush albums. Why matter does this is unclear, but it is evident that matter has Plans.

It is also apparent that creators sometimes favor the Big Bang method of universe construction, and at other times use the more gentle methods of Continuous Creation. This follows studies by cosmotherapists which have revealed that the violence of the Big Bang can give a universe serious psychological problems when it gets older.

Well, it was a start.

There was another pop, which left a small white shirt-button spinning gently in the vacuum.

Death relaxed a little. Of course, it was going to take some time. There was going to be an interlude before all this got complicated enough to produce gas clouds, galaxies, planets and continents, let alone tiny corkscrew-shaped things wiggling around in slimy pools and wondering whether evolution was worth all the bother of growing fins and legs and things. But it indicated the start of an unstoppable trend.

All he had to do was be patient, and he was good at that. Pretty soon there'd be living creatures, developing like mad, running and laughing in the new sunlight. Growing tired. Growing old.

Death sat back. He could wait.

Whenever they needed him, he'd be there.

The Universe came into being.

Any created-again cosmogonist will tell you that all the interesting stuff happened in the first couple of minutes, when nothingness bunched together to form space and time and lots of really tiny black holes appeared and so on. After that, they say, it became just a matter of, well, matter. It was basically all over bar the microwave radiation.

Seen from close by, though, it had a certain gaudy attraction.

The little man sniffed.

"Too showy," he said. "You don't need all that noise. It could just as easily have been a Big Hiss, or a bit of music."

"Could it?" said Rincewind.

"Yeah, and it looked pretty iffy around the two picosecond mark. Definitely a bit of ropey filling-in. But that's how it goes these days. No craftsmanship. When I was a lad it took *days* to make a universe. You could take a bit of pride in it. Now they just throw it together and it's back on the lorry and away. And, you know what?"

"No?" said Rincewind weakly.

"They pinches stuff off the site. They finds someone nearby who wants to expand their universe a bit, next thing you know they've had it away with a bunch of firmament and flogged it for an extension somewhere."

Rincewind stared at him.

"Who *are* you?"

The man took the pencil from behind his ear and looked reflectively at the space around Rincewind. "I makes things," he said.

"What sort of things?"

"What sort of things would you like?"

"You're the *Creator*?"

The little man looked very embarrassed. "Not the. Not *the*. Just *a*. I don't contract for the big stuff, the stars, the gas giants, the pulsars and so on. I just specialize in what you might call the bespoke trade." He gave them a look of defiant pride. "I do all my own trees, you know," he confided. "Craftsmanship. Takes years to learn how to make a tree. Even the conifers."

"Oh," said Rincewind.

"I don't get someone in to finish them off. No subcontracting, that's my motto. The buggers always keep you hanging about while they're installing stars or something for someone else." The little man sighed. "You know, people think it must all be very easy, creating. They think you just have to move on the face of the waters and wave your hands a bit. It's not like that at all."

137

"It isn't?"

The little man scratched his nose again. "You soon run out of ideas for snowflakes, for example."

"Oh."

"You start thinking it'd be a doddle to sneak in a few identical ones."

"You do?"

"You thinks to yourself, 'There's a billion trillion squillion of them, no one's going to notice.' But that's where professionalism comes in, sort of thing."

"It does?"

"*Some* people"—and here the creator looked sharply at the unformed matter still streaming past—"think it's enough to install a few basic physical formulas and then take the money and run. A billion years later you got leaks all over the sky, black holes the size of your head, and when you pray up to complain there's just a girl on the counter who says she don't know where the boss is. I think people appreciate the *personal* touch, don't you?"

"Ah," said Rincewind. "So . . . when people get struck by lightning . . . er . . . it's not just because of all that stuff about electrical discharges and high points and everything . . . er . . . you actually *mean* it?"

"Oh, not me. I don't run the things. It's a big enough job just building 'em, you can't expect me to operate them as well. There's a load of other universes, you know," he added, a slight note of accusation in his voice. "Got a list of jobs as long as your arm."

He reached underneath him and produced a large, leather-bound book, which he had apparently been sitting on. It opened with a creak.

Rincewind felt a tugging at his robe.

"Look," said Eric. "This isn't really . . . *Him*, is it?"

"He says it is," said Rincewind.

"What are we doing here?"

"I don't know."

The creator glared at him. "A little quiet there, please," he said.

"But listen," hissed Eric, "if he really is the creator of the world, that sandwich is a religious relic!"

"Gosh," said Rincewind weakly. He hadn't eaten for ages. He wondered what the penalty was for eating a venerated object. It was probably severe.

139

"You could put it in a temple somewhere and millions of people would come to look at it."

Rincewind cautiously levered up the top slice of bread.

"It's got no mayonnaise in it," he said. "Will that still count?"

The creator cleared his throat, and began to read aloud.

Astfgl surfed across the entropy slope, an angry red spark against the swirls of interspace. He was so angry now that the last vestiges of self-control were slipping away; his jaunty cap with its stylish hornlets had become a mere wisp of crimson dangling from the tip of one of the great coiled ramshorns that framed his skull.

With a rather sensuous ripping noise the red silk across his back tore open and his wings unfolded.

They are conventionally represented as leathery, but leather wouldn't survive more than a few seconds in that environment. Besides, it doesn't fold up very well.

These wings were made of magnetism and shaped space, and spread out until they were a faint curtain against the incandescent firmament and they beat as slowly and inexorably as the rise of civilizations.

They still *looked* batlike, but that was just for the sake of tradition.

Somewhere around the 29th millennium he was overtaken, quite without noticing, by something small and oblong and probably even angrier than he was.

Eight spells go to make up the world. Rincewind knew that well enough. He knew that the book which contained them was the Octavo, because it still existed in the library of Unseen University—currently inside a welded iron box at the bottom of a specially dug shaft, where its magical radiations could be kept under control.

Rincewind had wondered how it had all started. He'd imagined a sort of explosion in reverse, with interstellar gases roaring together to form Great A'Tuin, or at least a roll of thunder or something.

Instead there was a faint, musical twang, and where the Discworld hadn't been, there the Discworld was, as if it had been hiding somewhere the whole time.

He also realized that the feeling of falling he had

so recently learned to live with was one he was probably going to die with, too. As the world appeared beneath him it brought this eon's special offer—gravity, available in a choice of strengths from your nearest massive planetary body.

He said, as so often happens on these occasions, "Aargh."

The creator, still sitting serenely in midair, appeared beside him as he plummeted.

"Nice clouds, don't you think? Done a good job on the clouds," he said.

"Aargh," Rincewind repeated.

"Something the matter?"

"Aargh."

"That's humans for you," said the creator. "Always rushing off somewhere." He leaned closer. "It's not up to me, of course, but I've often wondered what it is that goes through your heads."

"It's going to be my feet in a minute!" screamed Rincewind.

Eric, falling alongside him, tugged at his ankle. "That's not the way to talk to the creator of the universe!" he shouted. "Just tell him to do something, make the ground soft or something!"

"Oh, I dunno if I could do that," said the creator. "It's causality regulations. I'd have the Inspector down on me like a ton of, a ton of, a ton of weight," he added. "I could probably knock you up a really spongy bog. Or quicksand's very popular at the moment. I could do you a complete quicksand with marsh and swamp *en suite*, no problem."

"!" said Rincewind.

"You're going to have to speak up a bit, I'm sorry. Wait a moment."

There was another harmonious twanging noise.

When Rincewind opened his eyes he was standing on a beach. So was Eric. The creator floated nearby.

There was no rushing wind. He hadn't got so much as a bruise.

"I just wedged a thingy in the velocities and positions," said the creator, noticing his expression. "Now: what was it you were saying?"

"I rather wanted to stop plunging to my death," said Rincewind.

"Oh. Good. Glad that's sorted out, then." The creator looked around distractedly. "You haven't seen my book around, have you? I thought I had it in my hand when I started." He sighed. "Lose me

143

own head next. I done a whole world once and completely left out the fingles. Not one of the buggers. Couldn't get 'em at the time, told myself I could nip back when they were in stock, completely forgot. Imagine that. No one spotted it, of course, because obviously they just evolved there and they didn't know there ought to *be* fingles, but it was definitely causing them deep, you know, psychological problems. Deep down inside they could tell there was something missing, sort of thing."

The creator pulled himself together.

"Anyway, I can't hang about all day," he said. "Like I said, I've got a lot of jobs on."

"Lots?" said Eric. "I thought there was only one."

"Oh, no. There's masses of them," said the creator, beginning to fade away. "That's quantum mechanics for you, see. You don't do it once and have it done. No, they keep on branching off. Multiple choice they call it, it's like painting the—painting the—painting something very big that you have to keep on painting, sort of thing. It's all very well saying you just have to change one little detail, but which one, that's the real bugger. Well, nice to have

144

met you. If you need any extra work, you know, an extra moon or something—"

"Hey!"

The creator reappeared, his eyebrows raised in polite surprise.

"What happens now?" said Rincewind.

"Now? Well, I imagine there'll be some gods along soon. They don't wait long to move in, you know. Like flies around a—flies around a—like flies. They tend to be a bit high-spirited to start with, but they soon settle down. I suppose they take care of all the people, ekcetra." The creator leaned forward. "I've never been good at doing people. Never seem to get the arms and legs right." He vanished.

They waited.

"I think he's really gone this time," said Eric, after a while. "What a nice man."

"You certainly understand a lot more about why the world is like it is after talking to him," said Rincewind.

"What're quantum mechanics?"

"I don't know. People who repair quantums, I suppose."

Rincewind looked at the egg and cress sandwich, still in his hand. There was still no mayonnaise in it, and the bread was soggy, but it would be thousands of years before there was another one. There had to be the dawn of agriculture, the domestication of animals, the evolution of the breadknife from its primitive flint ancestry, the development of dairy technology—and, if there was any desire to make a proper job of it, the cultivation of olive trees, pepper plants, salt pans, vinegar fermentation processes and the techniques of elementary food chemistry—before the world would see another one like it. It was unique, a little white triangle full of anachronisms, lost and all alone in an unfriendly world.

He bit it anyway. It wasn't very nice.

"What I don't understand," said Eric, "is why we are here."

"I take it that isn't a philosophical question," said Rincewind, "I take it you mean: why are we here at the dawn of creation on this beach which has hardly been used?"

"Yes. That's what I meant."

Rincewind sat down on a rock and sighed. "I

think it's pretty obvious, isn't it?" he said. "You wanted to live forever."

"I didn't say anything about traveling in time," said Eric. "I was very clear about it so there'd be no tricks."

"There isn't a trick. The wish is trying to be helpful. I mean, it's pretty obvious when you think about it. 'Forever' means the entire span of space and time. Forever. For Ever. See?"

"You mean you have to sort of start at Square One?"

"Precisely."

"But that's no good! It's going to be years before there's anyone else around!"

"Centuries," corrected Rincewind gloomily. "Millennia. Iains. And then there's going to be all kinds of wars and monsters and stuff. Most of history is pretty appalling, when you look hard at it. Or even not very hard."

"But what I meant was, I just wanted to go on living forever *from now*," said Eric frantically. "I mean, from *then*. I mean, *look* at this place. No girls. No people. Nothing to do on Saturday nights . . ."

"It won't even have any Saturday nights for thousands of years," said Rincewind. "Just nights."

"You must take me back at once," said Eric. "I order it. Avaunt!"

"You say that one more time and I will give you a thick ear," said Rincewind.

"But all you have to do is snap your fingers!"

"It won't work. You've had your three wishes. Sorry."

"What shall I do?"

"Well, if you see anything crawl out of the sea and try to breathe, you could try telling it not to bother."

"You think this is funny, don't you?"

"It is rather amusing, since you mention it," said Rincewind, his face expressionless.

"The joke's going to be wearing pretty thin over the years, then," said Eric.

"What?"

"Well, you're not going to go anywhere, are you? You'll have to stay with me."

"Nonsense, I'll—" Rincewind looked around desperately. I'll what? he thought.

The waves rolled peacefully up the beach, not

very strongly at the moment because they were still feeling their way. The first high tide was coming in, cautiously. There was no tideline, no streaky line of old seaweed and shells to give it some idea of what was expected of it. The air had the clean, fresh smell of air that has yet to know the effusions of a forest floor or the ins and outs of a ruminant's digestive system.

Rincewind had grown up in Ankh-Morpork. He liked air that had been around a bit, had got to know people, had been lived in.

"We've got to get back," he said urgently.

"That's what I've been saying," said Eric, with strained patience.

Rincewind took another bite of the sandwich. He'd looked death in the face many times, or more precisely Death had looked him in the back of his rapidly retreating head many times, and suddenly the prospect of living forever didn't appeal. There were of course great questions he might learn the answer to, such as how life evolved and all the rest of it, but looked at as a way of spending all your spare time for the next infinity it wasn't a patch on a quiet evening strolling through the streets of Ankh.

Still, he'd acquired an ancestor. That was something. Not everyone had an ancestor. What would his ancestor have done in a situation like this?

He wouldn't have been here.

Well, yes, of course, but apart from that, he would have—he would have used his fine military mind to consider the tools available, that's what he would have done.

He had: item, one half-eaten egg and cress sandwich. No help there. He threw it away.

He had: item, himself. He drew a tick in the sand. He wasn't certain what use he could be, but he could come back to that later.

He had: item, Eric. Thirteen-year-old demonologist and acne attack ground zero.

That seemed to be about it.

He stared at the clean, fresh sand for a while, doodling in it.

Then he said, quietly: "Eric. Come here a moment . . ."

The waves were a lot stronger now. They had really got the hang of the tide thing, and were venturing a little ebb and flow.

Astfgl materialized in a puff of blue smoke.

150

"Aha!" he said, but this fell rather flat because there was no one to hear it.

He looked down. There were footprints in the sand. Hundreds of them. They ran backward and forward, as if something had been frantically searching, and then vanished.

He leaned nearer. It was hard to make out, what with all the footprints and the effects of the wind and the tide, but just on the edge of the encroaching surf were the unmistakable signs of a magic circle.

Astfgl said a swearword that fused the sand around him into glass, and vanished.

The tide got on with things. Further down the beach the last surge poured into a hollow in the rocks, and the new sun beamed down on the soaking remains of a half-eaten egg and cress sandwich. Tidal action turned it over. Thousands of bacteria suddenly found themselves in the midst of a taste explosion, and started to breed like mad.

If only there had been some mayonnaise, life might have turned out a whole lot different. More piquant, and perhaps with a little extra cream in it.

Traveling by magic always had major drawbacks. There was the feeling that your stomach was lagging behind. And your mind filled up with terror because the destination was always a little uncertain. It wasn't that you could come out anywhere. "Anywhere" represented a very restricted range of choices compared to the kind of places magic could transport you to. The actual traveling was easy. It was achieving a destination which would, for example, allow you to survive in all four dimensions at once that took the real effort.

In fact the scope for error was so huge it seemed something of an anticlimax to emerge in a fairly ordinary, sandy-floored cavern.

It contained, on the far wall, a door.

There was no doubt it was a forbidding door. It looked as though its designer had studied all the cell doors he could find and had then gone away and produced a version for, as it were, full visual orchestra. It was more of a portal. Some ancient and probably fearful warning was etched over its crumbling arch, but it was destined to remain unread because over it someone else had pasted a bright red-and-white notice which read: "You Don't Have To Be 'Damned' To Work Here, But It Helps!!!"

Rincewind squinted up at the notice.

"Of course I can read it," he said. "I just don't happen to believe it."

"Multiple exclamation marks," he went on, shaking his head, "are a sure sign of a diseased mind."

He looked behind him. The glowing outlines of Eric's magic circle faded and winked out.

"I'm not being picky, you understand," he said. "It's just that I thought you said you could get us back to Ankh. This isn't Ankh. I can tell by the little details, like the flickering red shadows and the distant screaming. In Ankh the screaming is usually much closer," he added.

"I think I did very well to get it to work at all," said Eric, bridling. "You're not supposed to be able to run magic circles in reverse. In theory it means you stay in the circle and reality moves around you. I think I did very well. You see," he added, his voice suddenly vibrating with enthusiasm, "if you rewrite the source codex and, this is the difficult bit, you route it through a high-level—"

"Yes, yes, very clever, what will you people think up next," said Rincewind. "The only thing is, we're, I think it's quite possible that we're in Hell."

"Oh?"

Eric's lack of reaction made Rincewind curious.

"You know," he added. "The place with all the demons in it?"

"Oh?"

"Not a good place to be, it's generally felt," said Rincewind.

"You think we might be able to explain?"

Rincewind thought about this. He wasn't, when you got right down to it, quite sure what it was that demons did to you. But he *did* know what humans did to you, and after a lifetime in Ankh-Morpork this place could turn out to be an improvement. Warmer, at any rate.

He looked at the door-knocker. It was black and horrible, but that didn't matter because it was also tied up so that it couldn't be used. Beside it, with all the signs of being installed recently by someone who didn't know what they were doing and didn't want to do it, was a button set into the splintered woodwork. Rincewind gave it an experimental prod.

The sound it produced might once have been a popular tune, possibly even one written by a skilled composer to whom had been vouchsafed,

154

for a brief ecstatic moment, the music of the spheres. Now, however, it just went bing-BONG-ding-DONG.

And it would be a lazy use of language to say that the thing that answered the door was a nightmare. Nightmares are usually rather daft things and it's very hard to explain to a listener what was so dreadful about your socks coming alive or giant carrots jumping out of the hedgerows. This thing was the kind of terrifying thing that could only be created by someone sitting down and thinking horrible thoughts very clearly. It had more tentacles than legs, but fewer arms than heads.

It also had a badge.

The badge said: "My name is Urglefloggah, Spawn of the Pit and Loathly Guardian of the Dread Portal: How May I Help You?"

It was not very happy about this.

"Yes?" it rasped.

Rincewind was still reading the badge.

"How *may* you help us?" he said, aghast.

Urglefloggah, who bore a certain resemblance to the late Quezovercoatl, ground some of its teeth.

" 'Hi . . . there,' " it intoned, in the manner of one who has had the script patiently explained to

155

him by someone with a red-hot branding iron.
" 'My name is Urglefloggah, Spawn of the Pit, and
I am your host for today . . . May I be the first to
welcome you to our luxuriously appointed—' "

"Hang on a moment," said Rincewind.

" '—chosen for your convenience—,'" Urglefloggah rumbled.

"There's something not right here," said
Rincewind.

" '—full regard for the wishes of YOU, the
consumer—,'" the demon continued stoically.

"Excuse me," said Rincewind.

" '—as pleasurable as possible,'" said Urglefloggah. It made a noise like a sigh of relief, from
somewhere deep in its mandibles. Now it appeared
to be listening for the first time. "Yes? What?" it
said.

"Where are we?" said Rincewind.

Various mouths beamed. "Quail, mortals!"

"What? We're in a bird?"

"Grovel and cower, mortals!" the demon corrected itself, "for you are condemned to everlast—"
It paused, and gave a little whimper.

"There will be a period of corrective therapy," it
corrected itself again, spitting out each word,

"which we hope to make as instructive and enjoyable as possible, with due regard to all the rights of YOU, the customer."

It eyed Rincewind with several eyes. "Dreadful, isn't it?" it said, in a more normal voice. "Don't blame me. If it was up to me it would be the old burning thingies up the whatsit, toot sweet."

"This is Hell, isn't it," said Eric. "I've seen pictures."

"You're right there," said the demon mournfully. It sat down, or at least folded itself in some complicated way. "Personal service, that's what it used to be. People used to feel that we were taking an interest, that they weren't just numbers but, well, victims. We had a tradition of service. Fat lot *he* cares. But what am I telling you *my* troubles for? It's not as if you haven't got plenty of your own, what with being dead and being here. You're not musicians, are you?"

"Actually we're not even dea—" Rincewind began. The demon ignored him, but got up and began to plod ponderously down the dank corridor, beckoning them to follow.

"You'd really hate it here if you was musicians. Hate it more, I mean. The walls play music all day long, well, he *calls* it music, I've got nothing against a good tune, mark you, something to scream along with, but this isn't it, I mean, I heard where we're supposed to have all the *best* tunes, so why've we got all this stuff that sounds like someone turned on the piano and then walked away and left it?"

"In point of fact—"

"And then there's the potted plants. Don't get me wrong, I like to see a bit of green around the place. Only some of the lads says these plants aren't real but what I say is, they must be, no one in their right mind would *make* a plant that looks like dark green leather and smells like a dead sloth. *He* says it gives the place a friendly and open aspect. Friendly and open aspect! I've seen keen gardeners break down and cry. I'm telling you, they said it made everything we did to them afterward seem like an improvement."

"Dead is not what we—" said Rincewind, trying to hammer the words into a gap in the thing's endless monotone, but he was too late.

"The coffee machine, now, the coffee machine's a good one, I'll grant you. We only used to drown people in lakes of cat's pee, we didn't make them buy it by the cup."

"We're not dead!" Eric shouted.

Urglefloggah came to a quivering halt.

"Of course you're dead," it said. "Else you wouldn't be here. Can't imagine live people coming here. They wouldn't last five minutes." It opened several of its mouths, showing a choice of fangs. "Hur hur," it added. "If I was to catch any live people down here—"

Not for nothing had Rincewind survived for years in the paranoid complexities of Unseen University. He felt almost at home. His reflexes operated with incredible precision.

"You mean you weren't told?" he said.

It was hard to see if Urglefloggah's expression changed, if only because it was hard to know what part of it *was* expression, but it definitely projected a familiar air of sudden and resentful uncertainty.

"Told what?" it said.

Rincewind looked at Eric. "You'd think they'd tell people, wouldn't you?"

"Tell them wh—*argarg*," said Eric, clutching his ankle.

"That's modern management for you," said Rincewind, his face radiating angry concern. "They go ahead and make all these changes, all these new arrangements, and do they consult the very people who form the backbone—"

"—exoskeleton—" corrected the demon.

"—or other calcareous or chitinous structure, of the organization?" Rincewind finished smoothly. He waited expectantly for what he knew would have to come.

"Not them," said Urglefloggah. "Too busy sticking up notices, they are."

"I think that's pretty disgusting," said Rincewind.

"D'you know," said Urglefloggah, "they wouldn't let me on the Club 18,000–30,000 holiday? Said I was too old. Said I would spoil the fun."

"What's the netherworld coming to?" said Rincewind sympathetically.

"They never come down here, you know," said the demon, sagging a bit. "They never tell me anything. Oh yes, very important, only keeping the bloody gate, most important, I don't think!"

"Look," said Rincewind. "You wouldn't like me to have a word, would you?"

"Down here all hours, seeing 'em in—"

"Perhaps if we spoke to someone?" said Rincewind.

The demon sniffed, from several noses at once.

"Would you?" it said.

"Be happy to," said Rincewind.

Urglefloggah brightened a little, but not too much, just in case. "Can't do any harm, can it?" it said.

Rincewind steeled himself and patted the thing on what he fervently hoped was its back.

"Don't you worry about it," he said.

"That's very kind of you."

Rincewind looked across the shuddering heap at Eric.

"We'd better go," he said. "So we're not late for our appointment." He made frantic signals over the demon's head.

Eric grinned. "Yeah, right, appointment," he said. They walked up the wide passage.

Eric started to giggle hysterically.

"This is where we run, right?" he said.

"This is where we walk," said Rincewind. "Just walk. The important thing is to act nonchalant. The important thing is to get the timing right."

He looked at Eric.

Eric looked at him.

Behind them, Urglefloggah made a kind of I've-just-worked-it-out noise.

"About now?" said Eric.

"About now I think would do it, yes."

They ran.

Hell wasn't what Rincewind had been led to expect, although there were signs of what it might once have been—a few clinkers in a corner, a bad scorch mark on the ceiling. It was hot, though, with the kind of heat that you get by boiling air inside an oven for years—

Hell, it has been suggested, is other people.

This has always come as a bit of a surprise to many working demons, who had always thought that hell was sticking sharp things into people and pushing them into lakes of blood and so on.

This is because demons, like most people, have

failed to distinguish between the body and the soul.

The fact was that, as droves of demon kings had noticed, there was a limit to what you could do to a soul with, e.g., red-hot tweezers, because even fairly evil and corrupt souls were bright enough to realize that since they didn't have the concomitant body and nerve endings attached to them there was no real reason, other than force of habit, why they should suffer excruciating agony. So they didn't. Demons went on doing it anyway, because numb and mindless stupidity is part of what being a demon is all about, but since no one was suffering they didn't enjoy it much either and the whole thing was pointless. Centuries and centuries of pointlessness.

Astfgl had adopted, without realizing what he was doing, a radically new approach.

Demons can move interdimensionally, and so he'd found the basic ingredients for a very worthwhile lake of blood equivalent, as it were, for the soul. Learn from humans, he'd told the demon lords. Learn from humans. It's amazing what you can learn from humans.

You take, for example, a certain type of hotel. It is probably an English version of an American hotel, but operated with that peculiarly English genius for taking something American and subtracting from it its one worthwhile aspect, so that you end up with slow fast food, West Country and Western music and, well, this hotel.

It's early closing day. The bar is really just a pastel-pink paneled table with a silly ice bucket on it, set in one corner, and it won't be open for hours yet. And then you add rain, and let the one channel available on the only TV be, perhaps, Welsh Channel Four, showing its usual mobius Eisteddfod from Pant-y-gyrdl. And there is only one book in this hotel, left behind by a previous victim. It is one of those where the name of the author is on the front in raised gold letters much bigger than the title, and it probably has a rose and a bullet on there too. Half the pages are missing.

And the only cinema in the town is showing something with subtitles and French umbrellas in it.

And then you stop time, but not experience, so that it seems as though the very fluff in the carpet is gradually rising up to fill the brain and your mouth starts to taste like an old denture.

And you make it last forever and ever. That's even longer than from now until opening time.

And then you distil it.

Of course the Discworld lacks a number of the items listed above, but boredom is universal and Astfgl had achieved in Hell a particularly high brand of boredom which is like the boredom you get which a) is costing you money, and b) is taking place *while you should be having a nice time*.

The caverns that opened before Rincewind were full of mist and tasteful room dividers. Now and again screams of ennui rose from between the potted plants, but mainly there was the terrible numbing silence of the human brain being reduced to cream cheese from the inside out.

"I don't understand," said Eric. "Where are the furnaces? Where are the flames? Where," he added, hopefully, "are the succubi?"

Rincewind peered at the nearest exhibit.

A disconsolate demon, whose badge proclaimed it to be Azaremoth, the Stench of Dog Breath, and moreover hoped that the reader would have a nice day, was sitting on the edge of a shallow pit wherein lay a rock on which a man was chained and spreadeagled.

A very tired-looking bird was perched beside him. Rincewind thought that Eric's parrot had it bad, but this bird had definitely been through the mangle of Life. It looked as though it had been plucked first and then had its feathers stuck back on.

Curiosity overcame Rincewind's usual cowardice.

"What's going on?" he said. "What's happening to him?"

The demon stopped kicking his heels on the edge of the pit. It didn't occur to it to question Rincewind's presence. It assumed that he wouldn't be here unless he had a right to be. The alternative was unbelievable.

"I don't know what he *done*," it said, "but when I first come here his punishment was to be chained to that rock and every day an eagle would come down and peck his liver out. Bit of an old favorite, that one."

"It doesn't look as though it's attacking him now," said Rincewind.

166

"Nah. That's all changed. *Now* it flies down every day and tells him about its hernia operation. Now it's effective, I'll grant you," said the demon sadly, "but it's not what *I'd* call torture."

Rincewind turned away, but not before catching a glimpse of the look of terminal agony on the victim's face. It was terrible.

There was worse, however. In the next pit several chained and groaning people were being shown a series of paintings. A demon in front of them was reading from a script.

"—this is when we were in the Fifth Circle, only you can't see where we stayed, it was just off to the left there, and *this* is that funny couple we met, you'd never believe it, they lived on the Icy Plains of Doom just next door to—"

Eric looked at Rincewind.

"It's showing them pictures of itself on holiday?" he said.

They both shrugged and walked away, shaking their heads.

Then there was a small hill. At the bottom of the hill there was a round rock. Beside the rock sat a manacled man, his despairing head buried in his hands. A squat green demon stood beside him, almost buckling under the weight of an enormous book.

"I've heard of *this* one," said Eric. "Man who went and defied the gods or something. Got to keep pushing that rock up the hill even though it rolls back all the time—"

The demon looked up.

"But first," it trilled, "he must listen to the Unhealthy and Unsafety Regulations governing the Lifting and Moving of Large Objects."

Volume 93 of the Commentaries, in fact. The Regulations themselves comprised a further 1,440 volumes. Part 1, that is.

Rincewind had always liked boredom, treasuring it if only because of its rarity value. It had always seemed to him that the only times in his life when he wasn't being chased, imprisoned or hit were when he was being dropped from things, and while falling a long way always had a certain sameness about it, it did not really count as "boring." The only time he could look back on with a certain amount of fondness was his brief spell as assistant Librarian at Unseen University, when there wasn't much to do except read books, make sure the Librarian's banana supply wasn't interrupted and, rarely, help him with a particularly recalcitrant grimoire.

Now he realized what made boredom so attractive. It was the knowledge that worse things, dangerously exciting things, were going on just around the corner and that you were well out of them. For boredom to be enjoyable there had to be something to compare it with.

Whereas this was just boredom on top of more boredom, winding in on itself until it became a great crushing sledgehammer which paralyzed all thought and experience and pounded eternity into something like flannel.

"This is dreadful," he said.

The chained man raised a haggard face. "You're telling me?" he said. "I used to *like* pushing the ball up the hill. You could stop for a chat, you could see what was going on, you could try various holds and everything. I was a bit of a tourist attraction, people used to point me out. I wouldn't say it was *fun*, but it gave you a purpose in the afterlife."

"And I used to help him," said the demon, its voice raw with sullen indignation. "Give you a bit of a hand, sometimes, didn't I? Pass on a bit of gossip and that. Sort of encourage him when it rolled back and that. I'd say things like 'whoops, there goes the bleeder again,' and he'd say 'Bugger it.' We had some times, dint we? Great times." It blew its nose.

Rincewind coughed.

" 'Sgetting too much," said the demon. "We used to be happy in the old days. It wasn't as if it used to hurt anyone much and, well, we was all in it together."

"That's it," said the chained man. "You knew if you kept your nose clean you'd stand a chance of getting out one day. You know, once a week now I have to stop this for craft lessons?"

"That must be nice," said Rincewind uncertainly.

The man's eyes narrowed. *"Basketwork?"* he said.

"I been here eighteen millennia, demon and imp," grumbled the demon. "I learned my trade, I did. Eighteen thousand bloody years behind the pitchfork, and now this. Reading a—"

A sonic boom echoed the length of Hell.

"Oi oi," said the demon. "He's back. He sounds

170

angry, too. We'd better get our heads down." And indeed, all over the circles of Hades, demons and damned were groaning in unison and getting back to their private hells.

The chained man broke into a sweat.

"Look, Vizzimuth," he said, "couldn't we just sort of miss out one or two paragraphs—"

"It's my *job*," said the demon wretchedly. "You know He checks up, it's more than my job's worth—" He broke off, gave Rincewind a sad grimace, and patted the sobbing figure with a gentle talon.

"Tell you what," he said kindly, "I'll skip some of the subclauses."

Rincewind took Eric by an unresisting shoulder.

"We'd better get along," he said quietly.

"This is really horrible," said Eric, as they walked away. "It gives evil a bad name."

"Um," said Rincewind. He didn't like the sound of Him being back and Him being angry. Whenever something important enough to deserve capital letters was angry in the vicinity of Rincewind, it was usually angry with him.

"If you know such a lot about this place," he said, "perhaps you can remember how to get out?"

171

Eric scratched his head. "It helps if one of you is a girl," he said. "According to Ephebian mythology, there's a girl who comes down here every winter."

"To keep warm?"

"I think the story says she actually *creates* the winter, sort of."

"I've known women like that," said Rincewind, nodding wisely.

"Or it helps if you've got a lyre, I think."

"Ah. We could be on firmer ground here," said Rincewind. He thought for a bit and then said, "Er. My dog . . . my dog has six legs."

"The kind you play," said Eric patiently.

"Oh."

"And, and, and when you *do* leave, if you look back . . . I think pomegranates come into it somewhere, or, or, or you turn into a piece of wood."

"I never look back," said Rincewind firmly. "One of the first rules of running away is, never look back."

There was a roar behind them.

"Especially when you hear loud noises," Rincewind went on. "When it comes to cowardice, that's what sorts out the men from the sheep. You run straight away." He grabbed the skirts of his robe.

And they ran and ran, until a familiar voice said: "Ho there, dear lads. Hop up. It's amazing how you meet old friends down here."

And another voice said, "Wossname? Wossname?"

"Where are they!"

The sublords of Hell trembled. This was going to be dreadful. It might even result in a memo.

"They can't have escaped," rasped Astfgl.

"They're here somewhere. Why can you not *find* them? Am I surrounded by incompetents as well as fools?"

"My lord—"

The demon princes turned.

The speaker was Duke Vassenego, one of the oldest demons. How old, no one knew. But if he didn't actually invent original sin, at least he made one of the first copies. In terms of sheer enterprise and deviousness of mind he might even have passed for human and, in fact, generally took the

173

form of an old, rather sad lawyer with an eagle somewhere in his ancestry.

And every demonic mind thought: poor old Vassenego, he's done it this time. This won't be just a memo, this will be a policy statement, c.c.'d to all departments and a copy for files.

Astfgl turned slowly, as though mounted on a turntable. He was back in his preferred form now but had pulled himself together, as it were, on a higher level of emotion. The mere thought of living humans in his domain made him twang with fury like a violin string. You couldn't trust them. They were unreliable. The last human allowed down here alive had given the place a terribly bad Press. Above all, they made him feel inferior.

Now the full wattage of his anger focused on the old demon.

"You had a point to make?" he said.

"I was merely going to say, lord, that we have made an extensive search of all eight circles and I am really certain—"

"Silence! Don't think I don't know what's going on," growled Astfgl, circling the drawn figure. "I've seen you—and *you*, and *you*"—his trident

174

pointed at some of the other old lords—"plotting in corners, encouraging rebellion! *I* rule here, is that not so? And I will be obeyed!"

Vassenego was pale. His patrician nostrils flared like jet intakes. Everything about him said: you pompous little creature, of course we encourage rebellion, we're demons! And I was maddening the minds of princes when you were encouraging cats to leave dead mice under the bed, you small-minded, paper-worshipping nincompoop! Everything about him said this except for his voice, which said, calmly, "No one is denying this, sire."

"Then search again! And the demon who let them in is to be taken to the lowest pit and disassembled, is that clear?"

Vassenego's eyebrows rose. "Old Urglefloggah, sire? He was foolish, certainly, but he is a loyal—"

"Are you by any chance endeavoring to contradict me?"

Vassenego hesitated. Dreadful as he privately held the King to be, demons are strong believers in precedence and hierarchy. There were too many young demons pressing below them for the senior lords to openly demonstrate the ways of regicide and coup, no matter what the provocation. Vassenego had plans of his own. No sense in spoiling things now.

"No, sire," he said. "But that will mean, sire, that the dread portal is no longer—"

"*Do it!*"

The Luggage arrived at the dread portal.

There was no way to describe how angry you can get running nearly twice the length of the space-time continuum, and the Luggage had been pretty annoyed to start with.

It looked at the hinges. It looked at the locks. It backed away a bit and appeared to read the new sign over the portal.

Possibly this made it angrier, although with the Luggage there wasn't any reliable way of telling because it spent all its time beyond, in a manner of speaking, the hostility event horizon.

The doors of Hell were ancient. It wasn't just time and heat that had baked their wood to something like black granite. They'd picked up fear and dull evil. They were more than mere things to fill a hole in the wall. They were bright enough to be dimly aware of what their future was likely to hold.

They watched the Luggage shuffle back across the sand, flex its legs and crouch down.

The lock clicked. The bolts dragged themselves back hurriedly. The great bars jerked from their sockets. The doors flung themselves back against the wall.

The Luggage untensed. It straightened. It stepped forward. It almost strutted. It passed between the straining hinges and, when it was nearly through, turned and gave the nearest door a damn good kick.

There was a great treadmill. It didn't power anything, and had particularly creaky bearings. It was one of Astfgl's more inspired ideas, and had no use whatsoever except to show several hundred people that if they had thought their lives had been pretty pointless, they hadn't seen anything yet.

"We can't stay here forever," said Rincewind. "We need to do things. Like *eat*."

"That's one of the tremendous advantages of being a damned soul," said Ponce da Quirm. "All the old bodily cares fade away. Of course, you get a completely *new* set of cares, but I have always found it advisable to look for the silver lining."

"Wossname!" said the parrot, who was sitting on his shoulder.

"Fancy that," said Rincewind. "I never knew animals could go to Hell. Although I can quite see why they made an exception in this case."

"Up yours, wizard!"

"Why don't they look for us here, that's what I don't understand?" said Eric.

"Shut up and keep walking," said Rincewind. "They're stupid, that's why. They can't imagine that we would be doing something like this."

"Yes, they're right there. *I* can't imagine that we are doing something like this, either," said Eric.

Rincewind treadled for a bit, watching a crowd of frantically searching demons hurry past.

"So you didn't find the Fountain of Youth, then," he said, feeling that he should make some conversation.

"Oh, but I did," said da Quirm earnestly. "A clear spring, deep in the jungle. It was very impressive. I had a good long drink, too. Or draft, which I think is the more appropriate word."

"And—?" said Rincewind.

"It definitely worked. Yes. For a while there I could definitely feel myself getting younger."

"But—" Rincewind waved a vague hand to take in da Quirm, the treadmill, the towering circles of the Pit.

"Ah," said the old man. "Of course, that's the really annoying bit. I'd read so much about the Fountain, and you'd have thought someone in all those books would have mentioned the really vital thing about the water, wouldn't you?"

"Which was—?"

"*Boil it first.* Says it all, doesn't it? Terrible shame, really."

The Luggage trotted down the great spiral road that linked the circles of the Pit. Even if conditions had been normal it probably would not have attracted much attention. If anything, it was rather less astonishing than most of the denizens.

"This is really boring," said Eric.

"That's the point," said Rincewind.

"We shouldn't be lurking here, we should be trying to find a way out!"

"Well, yes, but there isn't one."

"There is, in fact," said a voice behind Rincewind. It was the voice of someone who had seen it all and hadn't liked any of it very much.

"Lavaeolus?" said Rincewind. His ancestor was right behind them.

" 'You'll get home all right,' " said Lavaeolus bitterly. "Your very words. Huh. Ten years of one damn thing after another. You might have told a chap."

"Er," said Eric. "We didn't want to upset the course of history."

"You didn't want to upset the course of history," said Lavaeolus slowly. He stared down at the woodwork of the treadmill. "Oh. Good. That makes it all all right. I feel a lot better for knowing that. Speaking as the course of history, I'd like to say thank you very much."

"Excuse me," said Rincewind.

"Yes?"

"You said there's another way out?"

"Oh, yes. A back way."

"Where *is* it?"

Lavaeolus stopped treadling for a moment and pointed across the misty hollow.

"See that arch over there?"

Rincewind peered into the distance.

"Just about," he said. "Is that it?"

"Yes. A long steep climb. Don't know where it comes out, though."

"How did you find out about it?"

Lavaeolus shrugged. "I asked a demon," he said. "There's always an easier way of doing everything, you know."

"It'd take forever to get there," said Eric. "It's right on the other side, we'd never make it."

Rincewind nodded, and glumly continued the endless walk. After a few minutes he said: "Has it struck you we seem to be going faster?"

Eric turned around.

The Luggage had stepped aboard and was trying to catch up with them.

Astfgl stood in front of his mirror.

"Show me what they can see," he commanded.

Yes, master.

Astfgl inspected the whirring image for a moment.

"Tell me what this means," he said.

I'm just a mirror, master. What do I know?

Astfgl growled. "And I'm Lord of Hades," he said, gesturing with his trident. "And I'm prepared to risk another seven years' bad luck."

The mirror considered the available options.

I might be able to hear some creaking, lord, it ventured.

"And?"

I smell smoke.

"No smoke. I specifically banned all open fires. A very old-fashioned concept. It gave the place a bad name."

Nevertheless, master.

"Show me . . . Hades."

The mirror gave of its best. The King was just in time to see the treadwheel, its bearings glowing red hot, crash down from its mountings and roll, as deceptively slowly as an avalanche, across the country of the damned.

Rincewind hung from the pushbar, watching the rungs whirr past at a speed that would have burned the soles off his sandals if he'd been foolish enough to let his feet down. The dead, however, were taking it all with the cheerful aplomb of those who know that the worst has already happened to them. Cries of "Pass the candyfloss," drifted down.

He heard Lavaeolus commending the wheel's splendid traction and explaining to da Quirm how, if you have a vehicle which put down its road in front of it, just like the Luggage was in fact doing, and then you covered it with armor, then wars would be less bloody, over in half the time and everyone could spend even longer going home.

The Luggage made no comment at all. It could see its master hanging a few feet away, and just kept going. It may have occurred to it that the journey was taking some time, but that was Time's problem. And so, flinging out the occasional screaming soul, bumping and gyrating and crushing the occasional luckless demon, the wheel bowled on.

It smashed against the opposite cliff.

Lord Vassenego smiled.

"Now," he said, "it is time."

The other senior demons looked a bit shifty. They were, of course, steeped in evil, and Astfgl was definitely Not One Of Us and the most revolting little oik ever to oil his way into the post . . .

But . . . well, *this* . . . perhaps there were some things that were *too* . . .

" 'Learn from the ways of humans,'" mimicked Vassenego. "He bade *me* learn from humans. Me! The impudence! The arrogance! But I watched, oh, yes. I learned. I *planned*."

The look on his face was unspeakable. Even the lords of the nethermost circles, who gloried in villainy, had to turn their heads.

Duke Drazometh the Putrid raised a hesitant talon.

"But if he even suspects," he said, "I mean, he has a foul temper on him. Those memos—" He shuddered.

"But what are we doing?" Vassenego spread his hands in a gesture of innocence. "Where is the harm in it? Brothers, I ask you: where is the harm?"

His fingers curled. The knuckles shone white under the thin, blue-veined skin as he surveyed the doubting faces.

"Or would you rather receive another statement of policy?" he said.

Expressions twitched as the lords made up their minds like a row of dominoes falling over. There were some things on which even they were united. No more policy statements, no more consultative documents, no more morale-boosting messages to all staff. This was Hell, but you had to draw the line somewhere.

Earl Beezlemoth rubbed one of his three noses. "And humans somewhere thought this up all by themselves?" he said. "We didn't give them any, you know, hints?"

Vassenego shook his head.

"All their own work," he said proudly, like a fond schoolmaster who has just seen a star pupil graduate summa cum laude.

The earl stared into infinity. "I thought *we* were supposed to be the ghastly ones," he said, his voice filled with awe.

The old lord nodded. He'd waited a long time for this. While others had talked of red-hot revolution he'd just stared out into the world of men, and watched, and marveled.

This Rincewind character had been extremely useful. He'd managed to keep the King totally occupied. He'd been worth all the effort. The damn-fool human still thought it was his fingers doing the business! Three wishes, indeed!

And thus it was, when Rincewind pulled himself free of the wreckage of the wheel, he found Astfgl,

King of Demons, Lord of Hell, Master of the Pit, standing over him.

Astfgl had passed through the earlier stage of fury and was now in that calm lagoon of rage where the voice is steady, the manner is measured and polite, and only a faint trace of spittle at the corner of the mouth betrays the inner inferno.

Eric crawled out from under a broken spar and looked up.

"Oh dear," he said.

The Demon King twirled the trident. Suddenly, it didn't look comical anymore. It looked like a heavy metal stick with three horrible spikes on the end.

Astfgl smiled, and looked around. "No," he said, apparently to himself. "Not here. It is not public enough. Come!"

A hand grasped each of them by the shoulder. They could no more resist it than a couple of non-identical snowflakes could resist a flamethrower. There was a moment's disorientation, and Rincewind found himself in the largest room in the universe.

It was the great hall. You could have built moon rockets in it. The kings of Hell might have heard of words like "subtlety" and "discretion," but they had also heard that if you had it you should flaunt it and reasoned that, if you didn't have it, you should flaunt it even more, and what they didn't have was good taste. Astfgl had done what he could but even he had been unable to add much to the basic bad design, the clashing colors, and the terrible wallpaper. He'd put in a few coffee tables and a bullfight poster, but they were more or less lost in the overall chaos, and the new antimacassar on the back of the Throne of Dread only served to highlight some of its more annoying bas-reliefs.

The two humans sprawled on the floor.

"And now—" said Astfgl.

But his voice was lost in a sudden cheering.

He looked up.

Demons of every size and shape filled almost all the hall, piling up the walls and even hanging from the ceiling. A demonic band struck up a choice of chords on a variety of instruments. A banner, slung from one side of the hall to the other, read: Hale To Ther Cheve.

Astfgl's brows knitted in instant paranoia as Vassenego, trailed by the other lords, bore down on him. The old demon's face was split in a totally guileless grin, and the King nearly panicked and hit

187

it with the trident before Vassenego reached out and slapped him on the back.

"Well done!" he cried.

"What?"

"Oh, very well done!"

Astfgl looked down at Rincewind.

"Oh," he said. "Yes. Well." He coughed. "It was nothing," he said, straightening up, "I knew you people weren't getting anywhere so I just—"

"Not *these*," sneered Vassenego. "Such trivial things. No, sire. I was referring to your elevation."

"Elevation?" said Astfgl.

"Your *promotion*, sire!"

A great cheer went up from the younger demons, who would cheer anything.

"Promotion? But, but I *am* the King—" Astfgl protested weakly. He could feel his grasp on events beginning to slip.

"Pfooie!" said Vassenego expansively.

"Pfooie?"

"Indeed, sire. King? *King?* Sire, I speak for us all when I say that is no title for a demon such as you, sire, a demon whose grasp of organizational matters and priorities, whose insight into the proper

functions of our being, whose—if I may say so—
sheer intellectual capabilities have taken us to new
and greater depths, sire!"

Despite himself, Astfgl preened. "Well, you
know—" he began.

"And yet we find, despite your position, that
you interest yourself in the tiniest details of our
work," said Vassenego, looking down his nose at
Rincewind. "Such dedication! Such devotion!"

Astfgl swelled. "Of course, I've always felt—"

Rincewind pulled himself up on his elbows, and
thought: look out, behind you . . .

"And so," said Vassenego, beaming like a
coastful of lighthouses, "the Council met and has
decided, and may I add, sire, has decided unani-
mously, to create an entirely new award in honor
of your outstanding achievements!"

"The importance of proper paperwork has—
what award?" said Astfgl, the minnows of suspicion suddenly darting across the oceans of
self-esteem.

"The position, sire, of Supreme Life President of
Hell!"

The band struck up again.

"With your own office—much bigger than the pokey thing you have had to suffer all these years, sire. Or rather, Mr. President!"

The band had a go at another chord.

The demons waited.

"Will there be . . . potted plants?" said Astfgl, slowly.

"Hosts! Plantations! *Jungles!*"

Astfgl appeared to be lit by a gentle, inner glow.

"And carpets? I mean, wall to wall—?"

"The walls have had to be moved apart especially to accommodate them all, sire. And thick pile, sire? Whole tribes of pygmies are wondering why the light stays on at night, sire!"

The bewildered King allowed himself to have an expansive arm thrown across his shoulder and was gently led, all thoughts of vengeance forgotten, through the cheering crowds.

"I've always fancied one of those special things for making coffee," he murmured, as the last vestiges of self-control were eroded.

"A positive manufactory has been installed, sire! And a speaking tube, sire, for you to communicate your instructions to your underlings. And the very

latest in diaries, two eons to a page, and a thing
for—"

"Colored marker pens. I've always held that—"

"Complete rainbows, sire," Vassenego boomed.
"And let us go there without delay, sire, for I sus-
pect that with your normal keen insight you cannot wait to get to grips with the mighty tasks
ahead of you, sire."

"Certainly, certainly! Time they were done, indeed—" An expression of vague perplexity passed
across Astfgl's flushed face. "These mighty
tasks . . ."

"Nothing less than a complete, full, authorita-
tive, searching and in-depth analysis of our role,
function, priorities and goals, sire!"

Vassenego stood back.

The demon lords held their breath.

Astfgl frowned. The universe appeared to slow
down. The stars halted momentarily in their
courses.

"With forward planning?" he said, at last.

"A top priority, sire, which you have instantly
pinpointed with your normal incisiveness," said
Vassenego quickly.

The demon lords breathed again.

Astfgl's chest expanded several inches. "I shall need special staff, of course, in order to formulate—"

"Formulate! The very thing!" said Vassenego, who was perhaps getting just a bit carried away. Astfgl gave him a faintly suspicious glance, but at that moment the band struck up again.

The last words that Rincewind heard, as the King was led out of the hall, were: "And in order to analyze information, I shall need—"

And then he was gone.

The rest of the demons, aware that the entertainment seemed to be over for the day, started to mill around and drift out of the great doors. It was beginning to dawn on the brightest of them that the fires would soon be roaring again.

No one seemed to be taking any notice of the two humans. Rincewind tugged at Eric's robe.

"*This* is where we run, right?" said Eric.

"Where we *walk*," said Rincewind firmly. "Nonchalantly, calmly, and, er—"

"Fast?"

"You pick things up quickly, don't you?"

* * *

It is essential that the proper use of three wishes should bring happiness to the greatest available number of people, and this is what in fact had happened.

The Tezumen were happy. When no amount of worshipping caused the Luggage to come back and trample their enemies they poisoned all their priests and tried enlightened atheism instead, which still meant they could kill as many people as they liked but didn't have to get up so early to do it.

The people of Tsort and Ephebe were happy—at least, the ones who write and feature in the dramas of history were happy, which is all that mattered. Now their long war was over and they could get on with the proper concern of civilized nations, which is to prepare for the next one.

The people of Hell were happy, or at least happier than hitherto. The flames were flickering brightly again, the same old familiar tortures were being inflicted on ethereal bodies quite incapable of feeling them, and the damned had been given that insight which makes hardship so easy to bear—the absolute and certain knowledge that things could be worse.

The demon lords were happy:

They stood around the magic mirror, enjoying a celebratory drink. Occasionally one of them would risk slapping Vassenego on the back.

"Shall we let them go, sire?" said a duke, peering at the climbing figures in the mirror's dark image.

"Oh, I think so," said Vassenego airily. "It's always a good thing to let a few tales spread, you know. *Pour encouragy le—poor encoura—* to make everyone sit up and damn well take notice. And they have been useful, after their fashion." He looked into the depths of his drink, exulting quietly.

And yet, and yet, in the depths of his curly mind he thought he could hear the tiny voice that would grow louder over the years, the voice that haunts all demon kings, everywhere: look out, behind you . . .

It is hard to say whether the Luggage was happy or not. It had viciously attacked fourteen demons so far, and had three of them cornered in their own pit of boiling oil. Soon it would have to follow its master, but it didn't have to rush.

One of the demons made a frantic grab for the bank. The Luggage stamped heavily on its fingers.

The creator of universes was happy. He'd just inserted one seven-sided snowflake into a blizzard as an experiment, and no one had noticed. Tomorrow he was half-inclined to try small, delicately crystalized letters of the alphabet. Alphabet Snow. It could be a winner.

Rincewind and Eric were happy:

"I can see blue sky!" said Eric. "Where do you think we'll come out?" he added. "And when?"

"Anywhere," said Rincewind. "Anytime."

He looked down at the broad steps they were climbing. They were something of a novelty; each one was built out of large stone letters. The one he was just stepping on to, for example, read: I Meant It For The Best.

The next one was: I Thought You'd Like It.

Eric was standing on: For the Sake of the Children.

"Weird, isn't it?" he said. "Why do it like this?"

"I think they're meant to be good intentions," said Rincewind. This was a road to Hell, and demons were, after all, traditionalists.

And, while they are of course irredeemably evil, they are not always bad. And so Rincewind stepped off We Are Equal Opportunity Employers and through a wall, which healed up behind him, and into the world.

It could, he had to admit, have been a lot worse.

President Astfgl, sitting in a pool of light in his huge, dark office, blew into the speaking tube again.

"Hallo?" he said. "Hallo?"

There didn't seem to be anyone answering.

Strange.

He picked up one of his colored pens, and looked around at the stack of work behind him. All those records, to be analyzed, considered, assessed and evaluated, and then suitable management directives to be arrived at, and an in-depth policy document to be drafted and then, after due consideration, redrafted again . . .

He tried the tube once more.

"Hallo? Hallo?"

No one there. Still, not to worry, lots to do. His time was far too important to waste.

He sank his feet into his thick, warm carpet.

He looked proudly at his potted plants.

He tapped a complicated assembly of chromed

wire and balls, which began to swing and click executively.

He unscrewed the top of his pen with a firm, decisive hand.

He wrote: What business are we in???

He thought for a bit, and then carefully wrote, underneath: We are in the damnation business!!!

And this, too, was happiness. Of a sort.

Lost? Confused?

Need some help navigating the morass?

Dip into this handy travel guide and discover

THE WORLD OF

TERRY PRATCHETT

THRILLING ADVENTURE
(well sort of)

WONDROUS MAGIC
(when it works properly)

FLAT PLANET
(of course)

(It's a lot like our own...but different.)

The world of
TeRRY PraTChett

usually finds itself irresistibly represented by
Discworld—a flat, circular planet that rests on the
backs of four elephants, which in turn are standing on the
back of a giant turtle. Don't ask what the turtle stands on;
you may as well ask what sound yellow makes. This is the
backdrop for an intricate and delightful world that Booker
Prize–winning author A. S. Byatt hails as "more complicated and
satisfying than Oz," where every aspect of life—modern and
ancient, sacred and profane—is both celebrated and satirized,
from religion and Christmas to vampires, opera, war, and everything
in between.* Reading Terry Pratchett is the literary equivalent of
doing a cha-cha. It's exciting, it's invigorating, and those more
rhythmically inclined say it's got a good beat and you can
dance to it. Best of all, it's pure unadulterated, sidesplitting
fun. So isn't it high time you got away from it all by
visiting the Discworld? Don't bother to leave your
troubles behind. Bring them with you, because on
Discworld they'll look different and a whole
lot easier to cure.

* Opera and war often sound quite similar, of course...

A Brief Musing on **DISCWORLD**
(in theory and in practice)

DISCWORLD novels are, appropriately enough, about things on Discworld, but they have a tendency to reflect events or ideas from our world. In each case, subjects are covered in a distinctly "Discworld" way, but some of what's seen and heard seems to comment pointedly and very humorously on the lives lived in what we are pleased to call "the Real World." Discworld is definitely not our world but eerily resembles it, and the sheer contrary humanity of all the characters on this extremely flat planet is as challenging and hilarious as our own at its best and worst.

TERRY PRATCHETT himself sums it up best:

“The world rides through space on the back of a turtle. This is one of the great ancient world myths, found wherever men and turtles were gathered together; the four elephants were an Indo-European sophistication. The idea has been lying in the lumber rooms of legend for centuries. All I had to do was grab it and run away before the alarms went off.

There are no maps. You can't map a sense of humor. Anyway, what is a fantasy map but a space beyond which There Be Dragons? On the Discworld we know There Be Dragons Everywhere. They might not all have scales and forked tongues, but they Be Here all right, grinning and jostling and trying to sell you souvenirs.

Enjoy. **”** *

---

* He's also been known to describe it in *The Discworld Companion* as "like a geological pizza but without the anchovies."

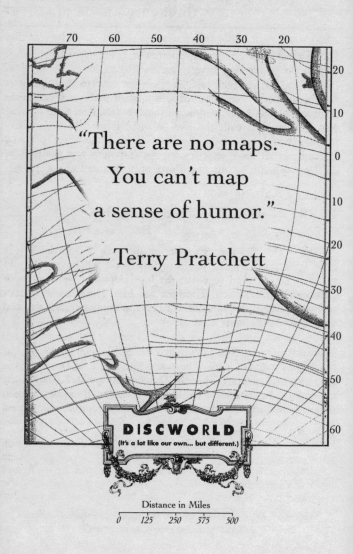

DISCWORLD "Map"

70 60 50 40 30 20

20

10

0

10

20

30

40

50

60

"There are no maps.
You can't map
a sense of humor."

— Terry Pratchett

DISCWORLD
(It's a lot like our own... but different.)

Distance in Miles

0   125   250   375   500

Some characters show up all the time in the novels of Discworld; others you may be hard-pressed at times to find. Any way you slice it, Discworld would be much more akin to a drab, uninteresting sitting room without this cast of heroes, villains, and assorted none-of-the-aboves.

So without any further ado, here's a taste of some of Discworld's finest whom you may run into from time to time. . . .

DEATH . . . An obvious sort of fellow: tall, thin (skeletal, as a matter of fact), and ALWAYS SPEAKS IN CAPITAL LETTERS. Generally shows up when you're dead, or just when he thinks you ought to be. Not a bad chap when you get to know him (and sooner or later, everyone gets to know him).

CARROT IRONFOUNDERSSON . . . Captain of Ankh-Morpork's City Watch police force. Bulging with muscles, this six-foot-six-inch dwarf (he was adopted) remains honest, good-natured, and honorable despite the city's best efforts. Carrot may also be the true heir to Ankh-Morpork's throne (a subject filed under "I wouldn't ask if I were you").

COMMANDER SAMUEL VIMES . . . Head of Ankh-Morpork's City Watch, despite his best efforts to the contrary. A slightly tarnished walker along mean streets, and like all good cops knows exactly when it's time to be a bad cop.

CORPORAL C. W. ST. J. NOBBS . . . Call him "Nobby"—everyone else does. Looking sufficiently like a monkey to have to bear a written testimonial as to his actual species, this City Watch member has a known affinity for thievery—namely, anything that isn't nailed down is his (and anything that can be pried loose is not considered nailed down). But honest about the big things (i.e., the ones too heavy to lift).

ANGUA . . . Now a sergeant in Ankh-Morpork's City Watch (which has a very good affirmative-action policy; they'll take anyone except vampires). She is a werewolf at full moon, a vegetarian for the rest of the month. Her ability to smell colors and rip out a man's throat if she so chooses serve as useful job skills, and have done wonders for her arrest record if not for her social life. A definite K-9 cop.

The **GANG**'s all there!

ESMERELDA "GRANNY" WEATHERWAX . . . The greatest witch on all of Discworld, at least in her opinion. Lives in the village of Bad Ass in the kingdom of Lancre (the village was named after a legendarily disobedient donkey, since you ask). A bad witch by inclination but a good witch by instinct, Granny prefers to achieve by psychology, trickery, and guile what others prefer to achieve by simple spells. She's someone to have on your side, because believe us, it's better than the alternative. Owner of a rather temperamental broom now made up entirely of spare parts. Any questions?

GYTHA "NANNY" OGG . . . The broad-minded, understanding, and grandmotherly matriarch of a somewhat extensive family, with fifteen children and countless grandchildren. She's had many husbands (and was married to three of them). Very knowledgeable on matters of the heart and associated organs. Likes a drink. Likes another drink. Likes a third drink. Make that a double, will you? She is the second member of the coven, which has included:

MAGRAT GARLICK . . . Once a witch, now the Queen of the kingdom of Lancre, this young witch doesn't adhere to the "old school" of witchcraft. She believes in crystals and candles and being nice to people—but she is a witch, so in a tight corner will fight like a cat...

and AGNES NITT . . . and while you're at it, why not meet Perdita as well? A witch with a split personality, the rather overweight Agnes Nitt walks the Discworld while Perdita (the "thin" person said to be within every fat one) whiles away her time daydreaming and offering unwanted advice and criticism. Gifted with an incredibly beautiful singing voice capable of any pitch or sound (comes in handy for belting out an aria in perfect harmony with herself).

MUSTRUM RIDCULLY . . . The Archchancellor of Unseen University. The longest-standing head of the University, Ridcully is notorious for his ironclad decision-making, the incredible lapse of time it takes to explain something to him, and his all-purpose wizarding hat (suitable for emergency shelter and the storage of alcohol). Is now ever more terrifying since he read a book on how to be a dynamic manager in one minute.

RINCEWIND . . . Simply put, the most inept wizard to ever exist in any universe. Rincewind possesses a survival instinct that far outweighs his spellcasting, and is such a coward that (if Einstein is right) he's coming back from the other direction as a hero. Guaranteed to solve every minor problem by turning it into a major disaster.

THE LIBRARIAN . . . It's the primary function of the Librarian of Unseen University to keep people from using the books, lest they wear out from all that reading. It also happens to be a primate function, given the fact that he's also a 300-lb. orangutan (transformed by a magic spell, but he prefers it so much he refuses to be re-transformed). Don't ever call him a monkey. *Ever.*

LORD HAVELOCK VETINARI . . . The supreme ruler of Ankh-Morpork. A keen believer in the principle of One Man, One Vote; he is the Man, so he's got the vote. Always in complete control of every situation he finds himself in, Lord Vetinari's sense of leadership and stability keep the city up and running...and you'd better believe that this is at the forefront of his mind at all times.

CUT-ME-OWN-THROAT DIBBLER . . . Not really a criminal, more of an entrepreneur who fits the needs of the times. Usually seen selling some kind of food in a bun (no matter how questionable its origins), C.M.O.T. Dibbler is always on the lookout for Discworld's latest business opportunity (again, no matter how questionable its origins). Not a man who asks questions, in fact, and he would prefer if you would also keep off ones like "what's in this sausage?"

COHEN THE BARBARIAN . . . The greatest hero in the history of Discworld. He's an old man now, but hasn't let that stop him. Don't laugh at him. In one of the most dangerous professions in the world, he has survived to be very, very old. Get the point?

THE LUGGAGE . . . Know it. Love it. Fear it. Constructed of magical sapient pearwood, the Luggage is a suitcase with lots of little legs, completely faithful to its owner, and completely homicidal to anyone it perceives as a threat to said owner. Baggage with a nasty overbite. Definitely *not* your standard carry-on.

THE GREAT A'TUIN . . . The gigantic space turtle upon which the entire Discworld rests (with four elephants sandwiched in between, of course). What is it really? How did it get there? Where is it going? (Actually, it is the only creature in the universe that knows *exactly* where it is going).

DISCWORLD on $30 a Day

This is quite easy to do, provided you don't eat and like sleeping out of doors. There are about four continents on Discworld:*

THE (UNNAMED) CONTINENT
Includes Ankh-Morpork, the Ramtops region, the witches' haven of Lancre, and the mysterious vampire-ridden domain of Überwald, whose fragmentation into smaller states after the breakup of the Evil Empire is occupying a lot of politicians' minds (anything strike you as familiar?).

THE COUNTERWEIGHT CONTINENT
Home to the fruitful, multiplying, and extremely rich Agatean Empire. Has a certain "Far East" flavor, with a side order of Hot and Sour soup.

KLATCH
Not loosely based on Africa at all. Honestly.

XXXX
A mysterious place to be certain, but some of its secrets have since spilled forth in the novel *The Last Continent* (by the way, "XXXX" is the manner in which it's written on the maps, since no one knew what it was supposed to be called). A vast dry red continent, where water is so scarce everyone has to drink beer. Still, no worries, eh?

---

* According to Terry Pratchett in *The Discworld Companion*, "there have been other continents, which have sunk, blown up, or simply disappeared. This sort of thing happens all the time, even on the best-regulated planets."

ANKH-MORPORK

> **"**There's a saying that all roads lead to Ankh-Morpork.
> And it's wrong. All roads lead away from Ankh-Morpork,
> but sometimes people just walk along them the wrong way.**"**
> —Terry Pratchett

Welcome to Ankh-Morpork, Discworld's most happening city and so carefully described it could be considered a character in its own right. Divided in two by the River Ankh—a waterway so thick with silt that it should really be considered a walkway instead,* Ankh-Morpork is one of those rather large cosmopolitan burgs that, like a lot of others with a similar claim to fame, always seems on the move but never really goes anywhere.

TAVERNS
Some of the many watering holes you can frequent on Discworld, where revelers can go in as men, and come out still men but with fewer teeth:

The Mended Drum
Originally known as The Broken Drum ("you can't beat it") before the fire, The Mended Drum ("you can get beaten") is hailed as the most reputable disreputable tavern on Discworld, where the beer is, well, supposedly beer (more colorful metaphors may apply). It's also here that you'll find some of the best in live entertainment that Ankh-Morpork has to offer . . . if getting slammed over the head with something heavy or a single serving of knuckle sandwich is your idea of fun.

Other pubs of (dis)interest: The Bucket; Bunch of Grapes; Crimson Leech; Stab in the Back; King's Head; Quene's Head; Duke's Head; Troll's Head (perfect for those with a death wish because it's still attached to the troll).

---

* "They say that it is hard to drown in the Ankh, but easy to suffocate."
—Terry Pratchett, *The Discworld Companion*

THE SHADES

Choose your path around Ankh-Morpork carefully, as you do *not* want to end up in the Shades. The oldest part of the city and about a ten-minute walk from Unseen University, the Shades is a yawning black pit with buildings and streets, an urban canker sore festering with criminal activity, immorality, and other similarly nasty habits. Every city has one. Need help? Don't expect any bleeding hearts around these parts, with the exception of your own. Multiple stab wounds can *hurt*.

THE PATRICIAN'S PALACE

Lord Vetinari's pleasure dome, complete with dungeons, scorpion pits, and other various forms of entertainment. The Palace Grounds are a must-see. Besides the obligatory bird garden, zoo, and racehorse stable, the Gardens, designed by the blissfully incompetent landscaper Bergholt Stuttley ("Bloody Stupid") Johnson, highlight a garden maze so minuscule that visitors lose their way looking for it, a trout lake 150 yards long and 1 inch wide (perfect for the dieting fish), and a chiming sundial best avoided at noon (it tends to explode).

UNSEEN UNIVERSITY

Welcome to Discworld's most prestigious (i.e. only) school of higher learning and the heart of Ankh-Morpork. Think of it as a wizard's college and chief learning center of the occult on Discworld, dedicated to serious drinking and really big dinners.

The wizards don't so much use magic as not use it, but in a dynamic way (a bit like the atomic bomb) and the time not spent eating is mostly taken up by interdepartmental squabbles (which of course never happen in *real* universities).

Be sure to visit the Library, if the Librarian allows you in, that is (hint: bananas will get you everywhere). Once inside, gaze in wild wonder at its violation of physics with seemingly endless rows and shelves of tomes magical and otherwise—theoretically all of the books in existence, as well as those that were never written. Remember: no talking, no reading, no kidding.

School motto:

NVNC ID VIDES, NVNC NE VIDES

("Now you see it, now you don't.")

Terry Pratchett's DISCWORLD Trivia Quiz

1. Which book told us about the history of Roundworld through the model universe created in the Unseen University's High Energy Magic Building?

A. *Maskerade*
B. *The Science of Discworld*
C. *Hogfather*
D. *Feet of Clay*

2. In *Small Gods*, Brutha finds himself to be the Chosen One for which Great God?

A. Auditors
B. Om
C. The Great A'tuin
D. Tobrun

3. Ysabell grew up to marry Mort, Death's apprentice, and they had a child. Who is the child?

A. Carrot
B. Mustrum Ridcully
C. Susan
D. Lord Havelock Vetinari
E. Corporal C. W. St. J. Nobbs

4. Ankh-Morpork's most brilliant genius, he just doesn't know when to stop creating . . . is?

A. Leonard of Quirm
B. Rincewind
C. Ned Simnel
D. Corporal C. W. St. J. Nobbs

5. Which character in Discworld speaks only in capital letters?

A. Lord Havelock Vetinari
B. Death
C. Rincewind
D. Granny Weatherwax

6. Which dwarven member of the Watch has a proclivity toward wearing items of clothing and makeup (here's a hint, it's female)?

A. Miss Cheery Littlebottom
B. Miss Angua von Überwald
C. Miss Magrat Garlick
D. Miss Agnes Nitt
E. Corporal C. W. St. J. Nobbs

7. In *The Truth*, Mr. Pin snorts which items?

A. Mr. Dibbler's "hot dogs"
B. Powdered moth balls
C. Dog worming tablets
D. Sugar
E. Probably any of the above except maybe the hot dogs.

If you're stuck for answers (or would rather just cheat instead), turn to the last page.

THE PRAISE! THE ACCOLADES! THE KUDOS!

Oh, why not just skip the formalities and hoist Terry Pratchett on our shoulders for a job well done?

"Nothing short of magical. . . . Pratchett's Monty Python-like plots are almost impossible to describe. His talent for characterization and dialogue and his pop-culture allusions steal the show." —*Chicago Tribune*

"Pratchett has now moved beyond the limits of humorous fantasy, and should be recognized as one of the more significant contemporary English language satirists." —*Publishers Weekly*

"Offers more entertainment per page than anything this side of Wodehouse." —*Washington Post Book World*

"Gloriously uproarious . . . . Pratchett's humor is international, satirical, devious, knowing, irreverent, unsparing and, above all, funny." —*Kirkus Reviews*

"If Terry Pratchett is not yet an institution he should be." —*Fantasy and Science Fiction*

"Think J.R.R. Tolkien with a sharper, more satiric edge." —*Houston Chronicle*

"Discworld takes the classic fantasy universe through its logical, and comic evolution." —*Cleveland Plain Dealer*

"Truly original. . . . Discworld is more complicated and satisfactory than Oz. . . . Has the energy of *The Hitchhiker's Guide to the Galaxy* and the inventiveness of *Alice in Wonderland*. . . . Brilliant!" —A. S. BYATT

TEMPTED YET? How about enticed? Maybe pleasantly coaxed? Go on—but remember, once you read one Discworld novel you'll want to read them all. Here they are, then, conveniently listed in chronological order of events—and you don't even have to start at the beginning to get in on all the fun...

THE COLOR OF MAGIC
Introducing the wild and wonderful Discworld—witnessed through the four eyes of the tourist Twoflower and his inept wizard guide Rincewind.
ISBN 0-06-102071-0

THE LIGHT FANTASTIC
Here's encouraging news: A red star finds itself in Discworld's way, and it would appear that one incompetent and forgetful wizard is all that stands between the world and Doomsday.
ISBN 0-06-102070-2

EQUAL RITES
A dying wizard's powers were supposed to be bequeathed to the eighth son of an eighth son, but he never bothered to check the baby's sex. Now who says there can't be a female wizard?
ISBN 0-06-102069-9

MORT
Death comes to us all. When he came to Mort, he offered him a job. After being assured that being dead was not compulsory, Mort accepted.
ISBN 0-06-102068-0

SOURCERY
There was an eighth son of an eighth son. He was, quite naturally, a wizard. He had seven sons. And then he had an eighth son...a wizard squared...a source of magic...a Sourceror.
ISBN 0-06-102067-2

WYRD SISTERS
Granny Weatherwax was the most highly regarded witch of the witches' coven. But even she found that meddling in royal politics was a lot more difficult than certain playwrights would have you believe...
ISBN 0-06-102066-4

PYRAMIDS

Being trained by the Assassin's Guild in Ankh-Morpork did not fit Teppic for the task assigned to him by fate. He inherited the throne of Djelibeybi rather earlier than he expected (his father wasn't too happy about it either)...but that was only the beginning of his problems.
ISBN 0-06-102065-6

GUARDS! GUARDS!

Terror stalks the denizens of Ankh-Morpork. A huge dragon has appeared in the greatest city on Discworld, swooping from the sky at any time, day or night, charbroiling everything in its path. To the rescue arrives the Night Watch....
ISBN 0-06-102064-8

SMALL GODS

What do you do when your cup runneth over with little intelligence and a lot of faith, and your small but bossy god proclaims you the Chosen One?
ISBN 0-06-109217-7

SOUL MUSIC

Sure, there are skeletons in every family's closet. Just ask Susan Sto Helit, who is about to mind the family store a while for dear old Grandpa Death.
ISBN 0-06-105489-5

INTERESTING TIMES

The Counterweight Continent is in urgent need of a Great Wizard. They get the incapable wizard Rincewind instead. See him run away from war, revolution, and fortune cookies.
ISBN 0-06-105690-1

MASKERADE

Ankh-Morpork's newest diva (and wannabe witch) must flush out a Ghost in the Opera House who insists on terrorizing the entire company. Hint: that chandelier looks like an accident just *waiting* to happen...
ISBN 0-06-105691-X

FEET OF CLAY
A killer with fiery eyes is stalking Ankh-Morpork, leaving behind lots of corpses and a major headache for City Watch Captain Sam Vimes.
ISBN 0-06-105764-9

HOGFATHER
The jolly Hogfather vanishes on the eve of Hogswatchnight, and it's up to the grim specter of Death to act as a not-so-ideal stand-in to deliver goodies to all the children of Discworld.
ISBN 0-06-105905-6

JINGO
A nasty little case of war breaks out when rival cities Ankh-Morpork and Al-Khali both stake a claim to the same island. Not like anything that happens on Earth at all.
ISBN 0-06-105906-4

THE LAST CONTINENT
A professor is missing from Unseen University, and a bevy of senior wizards must follow the trail to the other side of Discworld, where the Last Continent is currently under construction. No worries, mate.
ISBN 0-06-105907-2

CARPE JUGULUM
The vampires of Überwald have come out of the casket, and this time they don't plan to be back indoors by dawn. They *love* garlic.
ISBN 0-06-102039-7

THE FIFTH ELEPHANT
Captain Vimes is Überwald's newest ambassador. His mission: to find the Scone of Stone and rectify the dwarves' succession problem.
ISBN 0-06-102040-0

THE TRUTH
Starting Ankh-Morpork's first newspaper is a bit harder than it seems. First your biggest supporter gets jailed, then there's the competition, but nothing is mightier than the pen in this satire on, well, the pen.
ISBN 0-380-97895-4 (hc) ISBN 0-380-81819-1 (mm)

COLLECT THEM ALL and watch your bookshelf jump up and down with uninhibited glee. Well, not *exactly*, because it's a bookshelf. But *you* will.

DISCWORLD TRivia Quiz Answers

1. B
2. B
3. C
4. A
5. B
6. A
7. E